Island of Tory

Regina M. Geither

Loconeal Publishing
Amherst

Island of Tory

Copyright © 2012 by Regina M. Geither
Cover Art © 2012 by George Peyton
Interior Image Art © 2012 by Alec Geither
Edited by Barbara Taft Verduccci

Loconeal books may be ordered through booksellers or by contacting:
www.loconeal.com
216-772-8380

Loconeal Publishing can bring authors to your live event.
Contact Loconeal Publishing at 216-772-8380.

Published by Loconeal Publishing, LLC
Printed in the United States of America

First Loconeal Publishing edition: March, 2012

Visit our website: www.loconeal.com

ISBN 978-0-9850817-0-6 (Trade Paperback)

Dedication

To Ron, Alec, Joseph, and Sean
Remember that dreams are the seeds of reality.

Table of Contents

Chapter One

I remember only fragments of the day my life was turned upside down and shaken into chaos. With little more ceremony than a child flipping a snow globe, my world changed. I can recall only a portion of the drive north; the landscape was a wash of dark green and dreary gray. The air even changed as we made our way closer to our destination. The smoggy city sky hung stagnant behind us. With each gulp we took of the salt-laden air wafting over the craggy shore, our lungs began to clear. The thought, however, of spending an entire month on a sparsely populated island off the coast of Ireland made my stomach churn. What would we do? What could we possibly talk about?

Both of my parents were college professors at Wexford University in Pennsylvania. Mom was a quantum physicist, and Dad taught theology. Our nightly dinner conversations revolved around the origins of life and whether or not there was a God. I remained neutral, trying not to think about a subject that seemed too distant from my teenage world, and every summer, they called a truce so we could "reconnect" as a family.

For my parents, the school year was always a flurry of essays to be graded and lectures to be given. For me, it was nine months of forced independence. I was actually fine with it most of the time. What teenager didn't wish their mother and father would take a more hands-off approach to parenting? I usually spent my abundance of unsupervised time reading, listening to music, or playing soccer, soccer being my absolute favorite distraction.

It was the summer's forced togetherness that killed me, as

if three months of unrelenting family time could make-up for nine months of living like a shipwreck survivor on a desert island. I mean parents can't have it both ways. Either they parent year round or don't at all.

"Arella, dear heart," Mom interrupted my wallowing, "I hope ya brought enough reading material for our stay. Aunt Fi's old cottage is pretty remote, and both your father and I have decided ta take the opportunity ta work on our books." Her voice was lyrical. She had tried to lose the Irish lilt of her youth, but to no avail.

Well, at least she was choosing to be consistent with her approach to parenting this summer. "Don't worry about me, Mom." I waved the volume of Irish fairytales I had picked up from the last bookstore we visited. "I'm prepared for any opportunity of boredom you can throw at me." I opened to the table of contents and let my eyes skim along the titles. Did I want to read about fairies, leprechauns, or magical lands with no escape? With an uninterested sigh, I slammed the book shut. I turned to look out the window, watching the blur of scenery speeding by until I started to get dizzy. I decided to close my eyes and take a nap. I planned on sleeping a lot this summer.

"El," Dad called to the backseat, looking at me through the rearview mirror, "There's quite a bit of history on Tory Island, don't ya know. There's an old lighthouse, some ancient ruins, and lots of legends." Dad's Irish accent was thicker than Mom's, but he never tried to hide it. In fact, he enunciated each word with a slow deliberate brogue that drew attention to his foreign pedigree like a neon sign. I knew it was because of the illness he had suffered as a boy.

When Dad was in his teens, he had fallen sick with an unnamed illness that wracked his body with feverish convulsions for a week. After five days, the doctors had washed their hands of him, advising my grandmother to begin making final arrangements. But then on the seventh day, his fever broke, and he began to recover. He was weak for several months afterward. Though his body finally regained its strength, his speech was left slurred. He often told me stories of how he would pray each night on his knees, begging for his ability to speak clearly to be restored. Then one day, it suddenly was...just like that.

"What do ya think, El?" my father persisted. "Ya game for a bit of explorin'?"

I eyed the shoulders of his tweed jacket, trying to imagine him exploring anything outside the pages of a book. "Sure, Dad." I rolled my eyes, hoping he caught my hint of aversion in the rearview mirror.

Even the name of our island destination invited reproach— Tory Island. I read somewhere that "Tory" was a term used for outlaws and bandits. I wondered if that was how the island was first settled. Had it been a holding place for outcasts and derelicts, society's rejects? Was it truly an island of Tories.

I began scanning a brochure I had picked up at the bookstore entitled *What to Do on Tory*. Yeah really, what? I frowned at the ruddy-faced islanders smiling up from the glossy pages of the pamphlet, looking so content in their lives of remote solitude. *Visit Balor's Fort. Attempt to make your dreams come true at the Wishing Stone.* Crimony! I tossed the brochure onto the seat next to me. This year was looking to be worse than most. At least last year there was a beach.

I lay down on the seat, concentrating on the feel of the tires' vibrations as they rolled over the N56 toward the port of Letterkenny where we would catch the ferry. I let my black hair fall over my face, a practice that drove my mother to madness, a habit I would intentionally never break. The straight, limp strands hid not just my billions of freckles but also my disinterest, which allowed me to withdraw without really leaving. This was my customary means of silent protest against all things disagreeable.

The hum of the engine and the motion of the car quickly lulled me to sleep. I can't remember anything else about the drive except its end. Out of total nothingness came the high-pitched squeal of rubber desperately grabbing pavement. I was violently jolted from my dreamless slumber as I felt my body suddenly flying off the seat. I heard another loud screech as my equilibrium was tossed in the air like a die, and then I felt myself tumbling end over end. Hysterical screams pierced the air inside the car; some were probably my own. Everything was dark as I felt my entire universe flip over and over. The sound of glass breaking and metal twisting spread panic through me, but I couldn't stop my body from rolling and bouncing. Everything was devoid of light, and as I was thrown through the darkness, my mind focused on one insanely ridiculous thought…Where was my book?

When my body stopped tumbling, everything was silent. Eerily silent. No crying. No screaming. No moaning. No more breaking glass. I wasn't even sure I was breathing until a pitiful whimper escaped from somewhere deep inside of me, "Mom? Dad?" The sound of my own voice scared me. I started to cry. That was when I felt the throbbing in my head. It felt like someone had put a vice around my skull and was slowly winding it tighter and tighter. Within seconds, the pressure was unbearable.

That was when I realized that my feet were above my head. I was wedged inside the car upside down. I felt around for the door's handle. Instead, I found an opening where I guessed one of the windows had been. My hands groped the edges of the hole. Something sharp poked my palms, and a stinging pain shot through my fingers and up my arms. My hands turned wet and slippery. My breath caught in my throat as I realized I was bleeding. I forced my body through the gap in the wreckage and rolled onto the ground.

The throbbing in my head subsided, and I stared into the darkness. I half wondered if I was blind. Everything was black. I couldn't see a shadow, the outline of our car...nothing. I tried to sit up, but I couldn't feel the ground. I couldn't feel my arms or legs. I just felt numb. No, not even numb. Detached.

I felt like crying again, but I couldn't. Was I dead? I suddenly began searching through my consciousness for a memory of what had happened. I didn't understand where I was. Panic shot through me. I felt the desperate need to escape.

That was when the first shadow appeared. It was just a pinpoint at first, a dark gray mass in the abyss surrounding me, but it grew larger and began to pulsate. I felt an inexplicable wave of terror pass through me. This thing was headed toward me, and it made my mind race with dread. I had no idea what the shadow was; still, I was scared of it.

The shadow triggered a memory of my parents at the dinner table. "When ya die, Deirdra," I heard my father say, "all of your past comes back ta ya, and ya must answer for the good or evil ya've done."

"Ya're wrong, Thomas," my mother had corrected. "When ya die, the energy of your consciousness leaves your body. There is no judgment, just death."

I had scoffed at their theorizing. However, as I lay staring at the growing shadow approaching me, I anxiously began to speculate on who was right.

The feeling in my limbs suddenly returned, and every one of my muscles began to shake with fear. It was then that I remembered tomorrow was my birthday. I would have been seventeen.

Chapter Two

I stared at myself in the full length mirror and scowled. I looked ridiculous. The plaid, pleated skirt was bad enough, but the white knee socks were too much. "I'm not wearing this!"

"Come now, Arella. Ya look beautiful, lass." Aunt Fi rolled the words off her Irish tongue so that I almost believed her. She winked one of her green eyes at me as she pulled the hem of my skirt so that the rolls at my waist came undone. "But Father Cillian will not be approvin' of these," she said holding my hand so that I was forced to look at my black-polished fingernails.

"With any luck, he'll throw me out. Then I won't be forced to dress in this idiotic getup."

"Ya mind your manners. Father Cillian was very gracious ta accept ya midterm. He understands your circumstances and wants ta help."

Help? How could anyone help? I started to feel dizzy as I forced the horrible memories of the accident to the back of my consciousness. "I don't want any help," I mumbled. "I'm used to dealing with things on my own." My neck and shoulders suddenly tightened, as this was my body's usual response to stress. Reflexively, my hand went to the pink scar on my right temple, the only physical reminder of that night. I bent my head to let my hair fall over my eyes. Aunt Fi brushed back the strands with a wrinkled hand. Her false teeth jutted out in a kindly smile.

I forced myself to return the gesture, but my lips quickly straightened. Out of the corner of my eye, I caught a flicker of movement just outside my aunt's room. I took an involuntary step into the dim hallway. The low ceiling and white washed walls of the narrow corridor closed in on me as my eyes squinted against the muted morning light. There was nothing there, just another consequence of that horrible night creeping into my attempt at normalcy, upsetting my hope to forget.

Aunt Fi put her arms on my shoulders and turned me toward her. I stared at her soft, round face and ruddy cheeks. If it were not for her gray hair pinned in a loose bun, she would resemble a little cherub. "Be it another shadow, love?"

I looked into her worried eyes and nodded, forcing myself not to let the tears break loose.

"Heed me, lass. These visions that ya be thinkin' ya see are nothin'. Nothin' that daily Mass and hours of prayerful studyin' won't fix. What ya need is ta keep busy so ya haven't the time ta worry 'bout seein' anythin'."

I lowered my head again, letting my hair veil my face. "Aunt Fi, you don't believe me, but I know the shadows are real."

"Sure I believe ya, dear. Sure. Sure." The old woman pulled me into her arms. She smelled like lilies and chamomile tea. I sighed as I closed my eyes, trying to block out the blackness that now vied for control of my mood.

✝ ✝ ✝ ✝ ✝

I walked to St. Colm Cille dragging my feet, wondering why anyone would choose to live on this rocky island. Tory was barely big enough to hold the four towns it contained. Aunt Fi's cottage was in An Baile Thiar or West Town. The majority of the homes and shops lining my route were all coated with a dingy whitewash, laying testament to the age of the village. An occasional pale yellow building broke the colorless monotony. The Academy of St. Colm Cille was situated just outside the town and was only a short walk through the narrow, dirt streets.

Good thing, too, because there weren't any cars on Tory. Everyone walked anywhere they needed to go.

One of the buildings I passed stood apart from the rest, thumbing its nose at the rest of West Town. My eyes were instantly drawn to its flash of color among the village's monochromatic backdrop. Its ugly façade was brilliantly hidden behind a bright paint job of orange and red, making it the obvious exception to the standard tedium of An Baile Thiar. I stood for a moment admiring it and the eccentric owner who had chosen to rebel against the uniform drab to which the rest of the town had succumbed.

I continued moving through the town, my black patent leathers pinching my toes tighter with each step. I kicked up the dirt trying to cover their hideous shine that screamed "new." Everything in this town was old except me. I was new and out of place, just like the paint job on the orange and red house. I would never fit in at An Baile Thiar or at the Academy. With any luck, Father Cillian would brand me a heathen and revoke his offer to admit me to St. Colm.

Aunt Fi told me that both she and my dad had graduated from St. Colm and that he would be proud to know I was attending. My heart twinged at the thought of my parents. I shook my head, dispelling the painful memories seeping back into my consciousness. Knowing I was never able to say good-bye was the worst. I was still in the hospital with my head injury when my parents were buried. My last memory of them was the back of their heads as they sat casually in the front seat of the car, anxiously awaiting a relaxing summer break that never came.

"Are ya lost?"

The lilting Irish accent caught me by surprise, though I knew I should only be shocked if I didn't hear one. I looked up to see a dark-haired boy staring at me with a crooked, gap-toothed grin. He was tall and thin, but his shoulders were wide. I shook my head and managed to say, "No, just new."

I hadn't realized that I was standing outside a pair of ancient looking oak doors bolted shut with huge iron hinges.

"Well, ya don't want ta go in there. That's where Father Dalbach resides, and he doesn't like ta be disturbed." The boy's smile was slightly mocking. "I'm Declan. Declan McQuilan. And ya're?" He extended his hand.

I awkwardly took his palm in mine and said, "Arella. Arella Cline."

"I don't mean ta be nosey, but we don't usually get foreign exchange students on Tory Island. Ya're from America, right?"

"Yeah," I blushed, "guess I can't hide that fact."

Declan laughed. His eyes squinted into little half moons, making his face come alive. "Why would ya want ta hide the fact that ya're American? Ya'll be a local celebrity, no doubt."

"I would prefer being anonymous."

"On an island this size, ya can't avoid bein' noticed."

I frowned, but Declan smiled. Shifting uncomfortably from one foot to the other, I crossed my arms over my chest, an unattractive habit I'd developed to ward off unwanted attention. Despite my best efforts, however, I could tell this boy wasn't going to let me wallow in my mire of self-pity for long. He continued asking questions despite my best attempts at being antisocial, "Ya said your name was Cline. Are ya related ta Miss Fiona Cline?"

"Yes, she's my great aunt. I'm staying with her."

"For the semester?" Declan's eyebrows raised in curiosity.

"Indefinitely." I hoped my abrupt answer would discourage Declan from further questioning, but it didn't.

"Where are your parents then?"

I felt my anger starting to simmer. "Gone. Car accident." I bit my lip and looked away.

Declan's voice softened. "My condolences. I wasn't meanin' ta pry."

"It's OK; I'm just still getting used to it."

Declan put his arm around my shoulders. "Come on, I'll show ya ta the registrar's office."

I shrugged free of his arm but offered up a weak smile as consolation. Declan didn't act slighted. He gave me another smile as he motioned me to follow him to the front of the stone building looming ahead.

The church and its school were two separate structures connected by a cobble courtyard. Both buildings were dauntingly large. I stopped in front of the church craning my neck to look at the bell tower. Its peak seemed to reach up right into the gray marbled sky. Just then the large tarnished copper bell began to chime.

"You better go, or you'll be late," I said turning to Declan with disappointment.

"The ruler 'cross the knuckles only hurts for a moment. I'm willin' ta take my chances." His eyes were twinkling with mischief, and I almost believed him. "I'm kiddin'. I'll have the registrar write me a pass. Someone needs ta show ya 'round the place, and first hour theology is not my favorite."

I smiled my thanks. "All right then. Lead the way."

"After ya, my lady," Declan said with a bow.

We climbed the limestone steps leading up to two massive doors. They were identical to the other door I had been looking at before, only much bigger. The oak planks were worn smooth with age, and the hinges creaked loudly as Declan ushered me through them. Our footsteps echoed loudly as we walked through the empty stone corridor leading to a small office.

"Miss Arella Cline needs her itinerary of classes, please."

The woman at the tiny desk frowned up at us through thick glasses. "Don't she know how ta speak for herself?"

Declan smirked before taking a step back, allowing me to approach the desk.

"My aunt, Fiona Cline, called Father Cillian yesterday to arrange for me to attend."

The woman at the desk looked me up and down, tisking disapproval. I kept shifting my weight from one foot to the other, trying to relieve my squished toes. The woman pushed herself up from her chair still staring at me. I tried to hide my polished nails behind my back, but I was too late.

The registrar's lips curled down in a harsh frown as she handed me a booklet. "Ya best be studyin' our dress code tanight along with the rest of your classes. I can see that the American schools are not as strict with their students as we are here."

I managed a "Yes, ma'am" just as she turned her back to rummage through a filing cabinet.

Declan wrinkled his nose and put his fingers to his face in the shape of a pair of goggles. I stifled a laugh with my hands. The registrar turned around. I immediately hid my hands behind my back and smiled as sweetly as I could manage without giggling.

The bell in the tower began to chime a second time. "Well, ya're already late for first hour theology." She handed me my itinerary.

"Excellent," Declan said. The registrar shot him a stern look. "I mean excellent that I can show her the way. I have first hour theology, also. Could ya write us a pass?"

The registrar grudgingly pulled out a pink pad of paper and scrawled her signature at the bottom of the top sheet. She stamped it with a loud click and handed it over with a sour smile.

Declan grabbed the pass with one hand and my arm with the other and pulled me out of the office. Our laughter echoed off the stone walls as we raced down the corridor and out into the cool, damp island air. Though the sky was gray, and it was starting to drizzle, there was a bright spot in my dark mood.

"You're terrible," I said gasping for breath between giggles.

"I'm terrible? Ya're the one breakin' dress code on your first day."

I crossed my arms and started to tap my foot while scrutinizing his open collar and loosely dangling tie. "I guess we both need better role models."

"Come on, let's get ta class before Father Cillian decides ta expel us both." Declan grabbed my hand again, and this time, I squeezed back.

We raced across the courtyard, splashing in the newly forming puddles. I felt my white knee socks absorbing the muddy water, and I was secretly glad. I tripped once, and the momentum of the fall sent me sprawling on my hands and knees. I landed on my hands in a pool of swirling rain water.

"Ya all right?" Declan asked as he helped me up.

"Yeah, it didn't hurt a bit." I did, however, expect my knees and palms to have some nasty scrapes on them, but they were just wet. "Stupid shoes."

"They're not made for runnin', ya know," Declan said with a wink.

"Thanks for cluing me in."

By the time we reached the school building, we were both wet and disheveled. Oh well, I was never great at first impressions.

The heavy door groaned open, and the heels of our dress shoes clicked noisily toward the room marked *Theology*. We both skidded to a halt in the doorway as the instructor stopped mid-sentence to survey his late arrivals.

"Well, Master McQuilan, happy ya decided ta join us

taday." The professor's face was expressionless, but his narrow chin and pointed nose made him look angry. He wore all black except for his white collar. A priest! I wrinkled my nose in distaste and then blushed when I realized the clergyman was looking straight at me.

"Right, well he's brought us a present anyway," shouted a red-haired boy with too many freckles.

"Quiet, Master Donland, or ya'll be joinin' Master McQuilan for evenin' penance." A chorus of jibes from the other students followed.

"Who 'ave ya found ta join us?" The priest was now eyeing me, still without expression.

Declan led me to the front of the room where the cleric stood on a small stage behind a podium. I felt thirty pairs of eyes zeroing in on me. I folded my arms across my chest and tried to keep myself from shaking.

Declan handed the pink pass to the priest and said, "Father Dalbach, this is Arella Cline. Arella, Father Dalbach." Declan's smile was wide. I looked at his eyes for reassurance and was set off balance when I realized they were a deep emerald green.

I fumbled to recover my composure while awkwardly offering my hand to the priest. "Pleased to meet you, Father."

Father Dalbach looked down his pointed nose without extending his hand and said, "Take your seats, please."

Declan led me to a seat in the middle of the room. I was glad he sat next to me. The seat was hard and uncomfortable, and it was awkward trying to keep my knees together. Damn this plaid skirt! I pulled the hem over my knees and gave up being lady-like.

Theology class was as boring as I thought it would be. Father Dalbach talked about original sin and venial sin and mortal sin, and I began to yawn. Someone behind me threw a wadded up paper at the back of my head, and when I turned to see who the culprit was, Father Dalbach glared at me. "Miss Cline, I am unfamiliar with the way classes are conducted in America, so forgive me if I don't understand how it might be possible ta learn when facin' away from the instructor."

I smiled my regret and propped my chin atop my stacked fists.

Forty minutes later the ancient copper bell delivered us from our boredom. Declan jerked his head to the door, signaling me to follow. We lined up at the narrow exit, anxious to be rid of the tedium of sin-ology.

"Hey, Declan, are ya in for taday's futbol match?" asked the red-haired boy with the smart mouth.

"Yeah, Colin, if Arella will play."

"Do ya play futbol, Arella?"

I bit my lip, knowing I would sound like a girly-girl. "No, I don't like getting tackled."

"Not American football, but real futbol," Declan corrected.

"Oh, you mean soccer." I blushed. "Yeah, actually I play forward, at least I did back home."

"Forward? What's that?" Colin asked crinkling his forehead so that his bushy red eyebrows nearly swallowed his blue eyes.

"She means striker," Declan explained.

Colin's eyebrows rose. "Ah, a lady striker. Cool."

"Yeah, we're in," Declan accepted for both of us.

Colin nodded and then faded down the corridor with the sea of students heading in the same direction.

Declan turned to me, "Let's see your itinerary then." I handed him the paper. "All right, looks like ya have history next. I have Gaelic, so I'll show ya the way and meet ya after."

"You don't have to." I felt guilty letting Declan walk me everywhere.

Declan smiled. His green eyes sparkled behind his messy

bangs, and I caught myself staring. "I know," he said breaking the spell, "but I want ta do it. That is, if ya want me ta."

I nodded, giving in to his sincere offer. Then I hid behind my hair.

We joined the students heading down the hall. We turned left down another corridor, and then Declan pointed to a large room lined with books. "I'll see ya after second hour."

I started through the door but stopped abruptly when I remembered I didn't have my class schedule. "Declan..." My words trailed off. He had already disappeared down the hall.

I entered the room which was unnaturally quiet. Though the floor was limestone, my footsteps were muffled by the volumes of books lining the room. A few of the students were leaning over their desks talking, but their lips moved wordlessly, their sentences swallowed immediately by the walls. I took a seat in the corner, and no one seemed to notice me. I was glad for that.

A bent old woman entered the room. She had a book in one hand and a cane in the other. Her shoulders were draped in a crocheted shawl made of gray wool yarn. Her tiny head reminded me of a gourd as it bobbed up and down with each step. Her white hair was pulled back into a severe bun at the nape of her neck, and she wore a pair of spectacles at the tip of her nose.

"Welcome. Welcome, students. 'Tis a glorious day." The professor's words rolled off of her tongue with a melodic brogue. "Please be so kind as ta open your books ta page sixty-two."

Reluctantly, I raised my hand. I really didn't want to call attention to myself, but I didn't have whatever book they were about to read.

"Yes, yes, dear?" The professor bobbed her head.

"I don't have a book." My voice croaked with

embarrassment.

"No book? How can that be?" The old woman's face was confused

"I'm new."

"New? Oh, a new arrival. I was informed that Fi Cline's niece was goin' ta join us. Would ya be her?"

"Yes, ma'am."

"Good, good. I'm Professor McAnnals." The woman nodded her head as she rifled through a drawer. She hauled out a heavy book, depositing it on her desk. A puff of dust rose into the air as loose papers spilled from the massive volume. "This is a much older edition than we are currently usin', but it'll have ta do."

Feeling too guilty to let the hunched woman carry the massive book over to me, I hesitantly left my seat to retrieve it. Again, I felt the discomfort of a roomful of eyes following me as I crossed the classroom. The book felt like it weighed twenty pounds. I was relieved to set it down on my desk, but not as relieved as I was to slide back into my seat.

I started leafing through the book, looking for page sixty-two. The yellowed pages were dry and brittle. Bits of the edges broke off the corners though I tried to be careful. I wasn't paying much attention to the pages I was flipping through until I turned to a page containing an intricate sketch. I half-heard Professor McAnnals begin her lecture, but I couldn't tear my eyes away from the illustration.

The sketch took up two entire pages of the text. It was a series of lines and swirls and hash marks. It looked like a maze, but there were symbols with labels in a language I didn't understand. Was it a map of some kind?

"Miss Cline, would ya read the next paragraph please." Professor McAnnals' words broke through my distraction.

I looked up, guilt coloring my face. I could feel the panic

cutting off my breath. Oh no, I could feel myself starting to hyperventilate. I shrunk behind my hair, hoping to disappear. A hand from the left quickly flipped my book to page sixty-two and pointed to the fifth paragraph. I began reading not really paying attention to the words I was saying. My voice was surprisingly steady.

"Thank ya, Arella," Professor McAnnals said as I finished the paragraph.

I looked to my left to see a girl smiling at me through a sprinkle of freckles. Her dark hair was long and braided down the length of her back. Her light gray eyes bubbled amiably.

"Thanks," I whispered.

She nodded still smiling and turned back to her book.

I half-heartedly listened to the other students. They were reading about the battle of An Cloigtheach or the Bell Tower. Apparently it was some kind of skirmish that took place on the island around 1595. Uninterested, I began leafing through the text again. Nothing in the book looked familiar, but then I was not ever into history anyway.

When the hour was up, I sighed in relief and rose from my seat to leave. A tug on my sleeve stopped me.

"When did ya arrive on the island?" chimed a high-pitched, baby voice. The girl with the braid was smiling at me again.

Her voice threw me for a moment, and I stared at her uncomfortably, saying nothing at first. After an awkward thirty seconds, I found my voice. "A couple of weeks ago," I said trying to excuse myself politely.

The girl reached out her hand, "I'm Brigid Dunn."

I took her hand and said, "Arella Cline."

"Are ya related ta Miss Fiona Cline?"

"Yeah, I'm staying with my Aunt Fi for awhile. I have to go. I have someone waiting for me." I tried to make my way to the exit, hoping Brigid would stop questioning me before she forced memories of the accident back to the forefront of my thoughts.

But Brigid followed closely, chattering her next question, "How long are ya stayin'?"

"Awhile."

"If ya like, I can show ya the island." The girl could not take a hint.

"Maybe." I was really trying to give her the brush-off politely.

"What made ya come ta Tory? We never get visitin' students here."

That was it. All of my muscles tightened. That was the question that hit a nerve. I turned to face the wide-eyed girl with the million questions. I tried to keep my voice devoid of emotion, but I heard it quiver. "My parents are gone. Accident. Aunt Fi is my only relative." There I said it! I felt the familiar dark cloud move over me. I blinked, resisting the urge to cry.

"Oh, I'm so, so sorry." Brigid seemed to be scrambling for the right words.

"Arella, ya've met Brigid?" Declan's gap-toothed grin was smiling in the doorway.

I quickly wiped my eyes before the tears had a chance to fall. "Yeah, we've met." I busied myself adjusting my skirt.

"I can take it from here, Brigid," Declan said. I could feel his eyes on me though I didn't look up.

"All right then. See ya at futbol?"

Declan answered, "We'll be there."

Brigid waved and disappeared into the crowded hall.

Brigid was playing too? I felt the sudden urge to uninvite myself. "About playing futbol today...I'm thinking maybe I should pass. It might be too much excitement for the first day." I didn't know if Brigid was a gossip, but I didn't want everyone at the game feeling sorry for me or whispering behind my back.

Two people being overly sympathetic toward my plight were enough for one day.

Declan put his arm around my shoulders. I stiffened at his touch, but I didn't try to shrug away this time. "Brigid's all right, a bit overly keen, but nonetheless a nice girl. And ya'll like the rest of the group, too."

I sighed aloud. "OK, but too many questions or understanding smiles, and I'm out of there."

"Not ta worry. The rest of the group will only be concerned with your futbol skills. If ya're good, ya could be from another planet, and they wouldn't care how or why ya came here."

"And if I'm not good?"

"Then ya'll have ta endure Colin's countless jibes and Brigid's well meaning assistance."

An unintentional smile slipped out. "All right, I guess it could be worse. What's next on my schedule?"

Declan pulled my itinerary from his pocket. "Physics."

A loud groan escaped my lips, erasing the smile. Declan chuckled and led me down the hall.

Chapter Three

When the bell for last hour dismissal rang, I hurried from my seat, anxious to be gone from the stone walls and echoing corridors of St. Colm. Declan was waiting for me just outside the classroom door. I smiled; it was great having my own personal escort through the halls of the Academy. It made my first day a lot less scary.

"How was philosophy class?" Declan's welcoming grin was twisted in sarcasm.

"Great, absolutely fascinating, that is, if you're trying to figure out the meaning of life," I answered.

Declan raised his eyebrows. "Well, aren't ya?"

"Are you kidding? All I want to figure out is how I'm going to make it through all of this reading," I said, nodding to the pile of books I was carrying.

"I could help ya." Declan's eyes lit up. "How 'bout after the futbol match? We have the same assignments. Studyin' with someone will make the time go quicker."

"Thanks, but I'm not much company when I'm doing homework."

Declan nodded. "All right then. Another time maybe."

"Sure."

He grabbed my pile of books and tucked them under his left arm, his own books stacked precariously under his right.

The sky outside the walls of St. Colm was threateningly dark. The clouds hung heavy overhead looking like a torrent of rain would burst forth at any moment. "I think a storm is coming. Maybe we ought to reschedule the futbol match," I said.

Declan laughed. "Ah, it always looks like rain here. If we only played when the sun was shinin', we'd never play at all."

"How can you stand it?"

"What?"

"The constant dreariness. Isn't it depressing?"

"Ya get used ta it, I suppose," he replied with a shrug. "What's the alternative?"

We rounded the cobble path leading away from the Academy's stone structures. I suddenly realized that Declan was leading the way. "Hey, how do you know the way to my aunt's cottage?"

Declan blinked. His face momentarily flickered with confusion before his expression changed to amusement. "Oh, I guess I forgot ta tell ya. We're neighbors. I live just down the road from your aunt's house."

"Really? Which house?"

Declan looked away before quietly admitting, "The orange and red one."

I grinned remembering how I had admired that particular house for being different. "That's fantastic! Were you born here?"

"No," Declan chuckled, "no one is born here."

"Why not?"

Declan's face turned serious, "Tory Island is a place ya end up, not a place where ya start out." My face must have betrayed my confusion because Declan quickly added, "It's not exactly the kind of place people pick ta start a family. Those who are able leave. Besides the Academy, there isn't much else ta the island, just some ancient ruins."

"Ruins of what?"

"There's an old hill fort, the remains of an old monastery, and some old graves. Nothin' too excitin'."

"Oh, I don't know; it sounds kind of interesting."

Declan's smile returned. "I'll show them ta ya if ya like."

"Yeah," I said, my curiosity peaked, "sounds like an adventure."

"How 'bout tamorrow?"

I accepted his invitation with an eager grin. "Sure."

We were already at my aunt's door. I took my armful of books, and Declan promised to pick me up for the soccer game in one hour. I looked up as the first drops of rain plunked down on my head. "Should I wear my boots and raincoat?"

"Only if ya're afraid of meltin'," Declan joked as he tucked his own books under his jacket and dashed down the limestone road.

I turned to the faded blue door of my aunt's cottage and jiggled the knob. The hinges protested loudly as I entered the mudroom. "Aunt Fi, I'm home."

"Well, Arella, ya look like ya've had a fine day." Aunt Fi smiled behind her wrinkles, her bun wagging with her head.

"Yeah, it wasn't too bad actually."

"Did ya make some friends?"

"A couple. In fact I'm going to play soccer-- I mean futbol-- with them in an hour."

Aunt Fi smiled, her false teeth clacking in her cherub cheeks. "I saw ya with the McQuilan boy."

"Yeah, he went out of his way to help me today. He seems really nice."

"He's a good boy." Aunt Fi kissed me lightly on the cheek. "I'm glad ya're makin' nice friends, lass. When I came here, the people were very welcoming. That's what makes this place so special. Once ya become bound ta it, ya would never think of leavin'."

"Bound to it?" What a weird thing to say. "What do you mean?"

Aunt Fi quickly covered her mouth with her hand like she

was trying to stop any more words from leaving her tongue. Her face went pale as she stammered, "Oh, ah, it's just an old island superstition. Nothin' a young girl would care 'bout."

Really? I tried a different approach. "How did you end up here? Declan says there's not much on the island except for some ruins and graves."

Aunt Fi's shoulders relaxed a bit. She licked her bright red painted lips and explained, "I came ta Tory rather unexpectedly. It was by accident, really. Ya might say it turned out ta be a happy accident." Aunt Fi winked. "Once Declan gives ya the grand tour, I'm sure ya'll see what I mean."

I smiled politely as I silently disagreed with my aunt. Looking out the rain-splattered windows of the mudroom, I couldn't imagine how anyone could fall in love with a soggy, remote, desolate island like Tory. Me? Bound to Tory? I don't think so.

I left my patent leathers under one of the windows and let an audible sigh of relief escape. I was finally able to wiggle my toes freely. In stocking feet, I slid across the floor's smooth oak planks through the small parlor and down the narrow hall. I dumped my school books on an empty telephone stand just outside my room. Aunt Fi's bedroom was just across the hall. My eyes were drawn to the wash of color emanating from inside. Almost every inch of every wall was covered by one of Aunt Fi's paintings. She was a watercolorist. How appropriate to work in a medium so reminiscent of the place in which you dwelled. Her works, though, were not dreary like the island weather. They actually were in sharp contrast to the surrounding climate. Each picture was a splash of vibrant pinks, radiant yellows, electric blues, and fiery reds. I shook my head wondering how the island of Tory could inspire such beauty.

The walls of my room were sparse. They were mostly bare except for the picture of my parents I had hung when I arrived.

The photograph had been taken on their twentieth wedding anniversary. I sat on the end of my bed and looked at the faces frozen in eternal cheerfulness. Dad's face had the same ruddy hue as Aunt Fi's, betraying a family history of favoring Irish whiskey over soft drinks. Mom's complexion was pale and smooth, almost angelic. The irony of that description hit me like a punch to the gut.

"Oh God, Mom and Dad, I miss you so, so much." I thought I was alone before, but now... I rested my head in my hands and before I could stop myself, my palms were full of tears. I couldn't decide if I was ashamed of crying or I was afraid of losing control, but I quickly sucked in my breath and stifled the avalanche of sobs starting to tumble. The faint scent of lilacs tickled my nose as I inhaled. My mother's perfume had always reminded me of lilacs.

Arella! Arella? We're here.

My head snapped up. What did I just hear? I looked around my stark room. My eyes flew to the picture. The faces in the portrait were frozen in silence, but the voices had sounded like my parents'. What was going on? Was this how you started to go crazy with grief? I knew the words couldn't be real, but the sound of their voices still rang in my ears. I clasped my fists to my ears, blocking out the insanity trying to move in.

Shaking my head, I got up from my bed and rushed to the bathroom. I turned on the cold water in the antiquated pedestal sink and splashed my face. I looked at my ghostly reflection in the oval mirror. Well, at least it was only my reflection I was seeing. Stress. The stress and anxiety of it all was finally catching up to me. I thought I was handling it, but I guess I was wrong.

I combed out my hair and pulled it into a ponytail before returning to my room. The picture on the wall was silent now. I was just being delusional, nothing more. I kicked off my uniform and threw it into the farthest corner of my room. Rummaging through an antique dresser, I found where I had stowed my soccer gear. A sigh of relief escaped my lips as I shimmied into an old pair of shorts and a t-shirt. After pulling a pair of long black socks over my legs, I slipped in my shin guards. Grabbing a pair of soccer cleats and a sweatshirt, I left the room.

Aunt Fi sat on a stool in front of a blank canvas in the living room.

"What are you going to paint?" I asked, leaning over her shoulder.

"Oh, I don't know yet. Ya see, it has ta come ta me. Sometimes it comes quickly, and sometimes it takes awhile. More often than not, it comes ta me when I sing. I like ta sing or hum the Gaelic tunes I was taught as a young lass." Aunt Fi waved her arm around the room at the collection of watercolors brightening the tiny room against the dim light pushing through the parlor windows. "Most of these I've painted ta the tunes of *An Mhaighidean Mhara (The Mermaid), Ar Érinn (For Ireland), or A Ghaoth Andreas (O South Wind)*."

"Would you paint one for me?" I asked almost in a whisper. I needed something else to look at in my room, something to take my mind off of things.

Aunt Fi turned to face me, "Of course, lass." She patted my hand then laid her left index finger against her nose in thought. She started to hum. The tune was beautiful and haunting at the same time. "Aye, I think it's just come ta me." She turned back to her canvas and started to apply a wash of blue to the top half of the blank canvas. Surprisingly, her gnarled hands moved skillfully from left to right, each stroke dismissing a portion of the canvas' emptiness, replacing it with a spray of color.

"What will it be?" I asked in hushed reverence.

"A surprise."

There was a knock on the door. I looked up to see Declan grinning through the wet windowpanes. "Oh, Declan's here already. I'll be home for dinner."

"Take your time an' enjoy yourself. I'll heat your meal when ya get home." Aunt Fi waved me on with paintbrush in hand, never looking away from her work.

I laced up my cleats and put on my sweatshirt as I slipped out the cottage door.

"Well, ya look like ya're ready ta teach us all a lesson," Declan said eyeing my well-equipped legs and feet. He wore a pair of worn leather shoes.

I smiled smugly. "Oh, you have no idea."

Declan's smile widened as he juggled a well-scuffed soccer ball from one foot to the other. "Ya played often in the States?" He passed me the ball, trying to catch me off guard.

"Often enough," I said as I caught the ball on the top of my right foot, sending it straight up and heading it back to him.

"Impressive. I guess I'll let ya play on my team after all," Declan teased.

"I'll have to see what the other team has to offer first," I countered with a grin.

"Ha! They're amateurs, the whole lot of 'em, but I'll let ya decide for yourself. Let's go."

Declan led the way down the dirt road. We jogged, passing the ball between us as we headed away from my aunt's cottage in the opposite direction of St. Colm. "How far is the field?" I asked.

"Why? Are ya gettin' tired already?" Declan exposed the slight gap between his front teeth as he mocked me. The imperfection made his otherwise handsome face genuine.

"Not a chance!" I kicked the ball past him on the left while racing around him on the right. "Back in the States, we call that *going around the cow.*"

"Oh, I'm a cow now, am I?" He ran faster to catch up with me. As easily as if I had passed him the ball, Declan swiped it away from my control and ran it down the road yelling, "Moo!"

I shouted after him, "Oh, I see how it is now. Just wait 'til the game."

The road started to descend slowly away from the whitewashed town toward a rutted field. Declan put his foot on top of the soccer ball to stop it from rolling down the embankment. I caught up to him, breathing hard. I tried not to let him hear me panting. Below, there were two makeshift soccer nets at either end of the grassy pitch; their crossbars and posts were made of rusty pipes, and the netting looked like they were old fishing nets. There was already a group of kids gathered. I recognized Colin Donland immediately, his red hair flagging my attention. Brigid Dunn was also there. Her neat braid bobbed with the rhythm of her dribbling feet. Some of the other players looked familiar, too. I recognized them from school, but I didn't know their names.

Thunder rumbled in the distance. I looked up at the dark sky swirling above and asked, "What if it starts to pour?"

"Then we'll get wet. I hope ya don't ruin your fancy shoes."

I looked down at my nearly spotless light blue cleats and then back up at Declan. "Don't you worry about my shoes. They've already been baptized in mud."

Declan smirked and jerked his head toward the others. "Come on then. Let's get the match started."

"Declan, Arella," Colin called as we jogged down the slope. "We've got enough for a game of 8 v 8 without subs. Let's divvy up."

"Who are the captains?" I asked.

"Ya and Brigid, since ya're the only girls," Declan offered.

I looked at the group of faces gathered around and realized

he was right; we were the only girls. "Sure, who picks first?"

Colin dug in his pocket. "We'll flip ta see. Arella, call it in the air." He tossed the coin high.

"Tails."

Colin caught the shilling with his right hand and slammed it onto his left wrist. "Sorry, it's heads."

Brigid did not waste any time. "I pick Declan." Her voice was giddy with triumph.

I was irritated immediately, but I tried not to let it show. "I'll pick Colin."

"Next I'll have Ulan," Brigid countered. Her smile had disappeared. She was suddenly all business.

It was my turn again, but I didn't know anyone else by name. Colin quickly came to my rescue. He whispered, "Sean. We need someone to play keeper."

"OK, Sean." A burly boy with dark hair and dark eyes stepped next to Colin.

Brigid looked annoyed, so it must have been a good pick. She quickly made an alternate choice, and it was my turn again.

"Connor or Keenan. We need some strikers with speed," Colin suggested.

"OK, Keenan," I announced without knowing to whom the name belonged. A small, wiry boy with sandy colored hair drifted over to join Colin and Sean where they stood behind me.

Of course, Brigid picked Connor next.

After several more blind choices, my team was complete, and we were ready to start. I didn't have to guess where to assign anyone. Everyone automatically migrated to their preferred positions. I put myself as left forward, next to Keenan. A tall, skinny boy named Joseph took right-wing. Colin positioned himself at mid. Sean, the burly keeper, shoved his large hands into a pair of gloves before planting himself in the center of the goalie box. His serious face reminded me of a warrior readying for battle. The three defenders, Kyle, Danny, and Bryce stood in a casual line, looking bored.

Brigid was handing out bright green pinnies while she organized her line-up. The clouds overhead began to swirl with more menace as the rain decided to pelt down on us. I swiped at the drops sliding down my forehead, trying to keep them out of my eyes.

"Don't worry. Ya won't melt, Arella," Colin called from his position.

"Thanks for the reassurance. I was worried for a second." I forced a smile as I tried to shake my damp shorts loose from where they clung to my legs.

"Ready?" Brigid called, squinting at me through the raindrops.

I gave her a thumbs-up. "We're good."

Brigid lightly nudged the soccer ball past the line. Declan, her team's right forward, took it and dribbled it straight toward me. Great, he was testing me already. I sprang forward to block him. I cuffed the ball with the outside of my right foot. The ball spun toward the center of the field. Keenan easily trapped it. He cut it back behind his body with his right foot and darted forward toward the goal.

"Yeah, yeah! Run up," Keenan urged, motioning me to follow his forward assault.

After running six feet, Keenan passed the ball back to me. I dribbled forward. Ulan, Brigid's midfielder, changed direction and headed away from Keenan and straight for me. I stopped, faked going to the left, and shot around him to the right. I carried the ball a few feet more before I was blocked again. Crap! Brigid was right there. She smiled smugly, her straight teeth too perfect and too white. I felt a flash of anger.

"Arella, ya got me back," Colin called from somewhere behind me.

I turned the ball away from Brigid and sent it flying in the direction of Colin's voice. Colin trapped it with the inside of his right foot and flashed me an impressed smile. Then his mouth drew tight into a concentrated line as he charged down the field with the ball. His feet moved so fast I almost forgot to run forward with him. I raced to catch up, my cleats kicking up clumps of wet turf as I went.

Declan ran back. He zeroed in on Colin and swiped the ball from him like the play had been choreographed. He dribbled toward me again. I glanced at his face. His dark, wet hair was pasted to his forehead, and his eyebrows were drawn together almost at a right angle. I charged toward the ball.

"Sorry, Arella, I'm not goin' ta be courteous twice," Declan called as he swung the ball from his right foot to his left and pushed past me.

Damn! I turned around in time to see Danny, our middle defender, block Declan's pass to Connor. The ball ricocheted off his shin back to where Joseph was waiting. Joseph settled the ball, took four steps, and sent it back up the field to Keenan. I turned around and scrambled to catch up to our charging strikers.

Brigid's right defender cut off Keenan twenty feet from the goal. He sent the soccer ball hurling back toward me. I jumped up to head it. I felt the beaten vinyl skim off the top of my head, but the ball did not change direction. Instead, I landed in the wet grass, my center of gravity slipping forward as I tumbled back. Before I could utter the curse word emerging on my lips, I landed with an abrupt bump on my backside, followed by a jolt to the back of my head.

"Arella, are ya all right?" I heard Declan's familiar voice.

I lay there for a moment, not moving. I couldn't decide what was going to be worse, the pain of the fall or the humiliation. When I heard the sound of clapping, I knew it would be the embarrassment. I slowly sat up, my skin instantly puckering into goose bumps as my sweatshirt and shorts sucked in the moisture that had puddled on the turf. I instinctively rubbed the back of my head. Hm, nothing. No bump, no pain. That was lucky.

"That was quite an impressive show of American futbol talent," called an unfamiliar voice.

All of the players circled around and stared down at me. Declan offered me his hand. I scrambled to my feet, brushing off my back and backside before anyone noticed the mud and grass stains that had accumulated there. I looked down at my feet, pretending to stomp my cleats free of divots. I could feel my cheeks burning with embarrassment. I undid my ponytail, letting my hair cover my face, fussing with it unnecessarily.

"What brings ya ta this part of the island, Cannon?" Declan asked the new arrival. "I thought the Academy and her members bored ya."

"Yeah, they do." The boy's voice was absent of the Irish brogue everyone else on the island possessed, and he sounded cocky and annoyed. I couldn't help but look up to see who was speaking with such unprovoked venom. The boy caught my look with his dark eyes and continued, "But, I had heard there was a new arrival, and I wanted to see for myself."

Declan smiled, but his lips slanted slightly down on the left, betraying his insincere congeniality. "Cannon Fidelous, this is my friend, Arella Cline." Declan looked at me ruefully. "Arella, please meet Cannon."

I nodded, but I couldn't speak. Cannon smiled. His dark eyes glinted with a hint of mischief as he pushed back the straight, amber locks hanging in his face. "Hello, Arella. It's a pleasure." He extended his hand.

I wiped my wet palm on a clean patch of my sweatshirt and muttered, "Hello," as we shook. He grasped my hand, and the sudden warmth of his touch sent a shiver of heat through my chilled bones. He stared at me, and I couldn't help but feel that we were already acquainted from somewhere else. He looked a bit older than Declan, maybe in his early twenties. His chin and cheeks were shadowed and unshaven. His skin was unusually tan for being a resident of the island. My eyes fixated on his. I knew I was staring, but I couldn't break the trance. Then his eyes moved to our clasped hands. He turned mine over in his, scrutinizing my palm. I felt like a slide specimen trapped between glass.

"If ya don't mind, we were in the middle of our game," Declan interrupted the spell. His usual cheery voice was edged with irritation.

Cannon continued to hold my hand and my gaze. "Could you use another player?"

"Sorry, sides are already even," Declan answered.

"Then I'll watch." Cannon released my hand as he crossed his arms and stepped to the sideline.

"No," Declan's voice was now angry. "We don't need an audience."

"Sure, but I've got nothing better to do."

Declan stepped toward Cannon, his chest puffed out and his chin set. "Piss off, Cannon. We're tryin' ta play our game, and we don't need ya hangin' around makin' snide remarks."

Cannon smiled coolly. "Why would it matter to you what I say? Come on; show me how real futbol players play the game. Teach me."

Declan stepped closer to Cannon. They were nose to nose. "Yeah, I'll teach ya." I saw Declan's hands flex in and out of fists.

"Boys, let's not fight now." Brigid's high-pitched voice cut through the tension.

Just then, a bolt of lightning zigzagged through the

churning sky. Immediately there was a loud crack of thunder. Before I could look up, the sky let loose a torrent of wind and rain. The drops that had fallen before were only a trickle compared to the deluge that now pelted our bodies.

"Sorry, looks like we'll have ta call it a day," Declan yelled above the sound of the storm. His smile betrayed his obvious satisfaction.

"Yeah, this island knows how to turn on the charm for sure," Cannon answered. "Arella, I'll be seeing you." He turned and walked away, not bothering to rush for shelter from the storm.

Declan grabbed my hand. "Come on, Arella." He pulled me back toward the direction we had taken to get to the field, kicking the soccer ball through puddles as we went. I looked back to say good-bye, but the others had already faded away behind the sheets of rain.

By the time we reached Aunt Fi's cottage, our clothes hung on our frames like wet rags. My cleats were tight and swollen with moisture, and I was sure I would have a blister on my left, little toe when I could finally peel off the soggy socks that were now molded to my pruning feet. I opened the door to the mudroom, and we both gratefully stepped out of the downpour.

"Well, that was interesting," I said, staring at the huge puddle forming on the mudroom floor.

Declan chuckled. "Better get used ta it. The sun hardly ever shines on Tory." My dismay must have immediately showed because Declan quickly added, "But, it doesn't always come down so hard. Usually just drizzle."

I couldn't force my face to brighten. How could anyone deal with so much rain? I faked a smile and offered, "Well, I guess I'll have to learn to play in the rain."

"That's the spirit. And tamorrow after school, I'll give ya a guided tour of the ruins, like I promised."

I nodded and smiled for real. Declan winked then turned to leave.

"Declan?" He turned back to face me. "Why don't you and Cannon like each other?"

Declan's face hardened and was suddenly devoid of emotion. "We're from different worlds."

"So are you and I," I offered.

Declan grinned, "Not any more we're not. See ya in the mornin', Arella."

I tried to watch him leave, but he was quickly swallowed by the weather.

Chapter Four

I waded my way through my second day of monotony at St. Colm's. Time dragged on with no relief from the boredom. The professors' lectures droned in my ears like the sound of an irritating buzz that refused to be silenced. Because more of the students seemed to be interested in me, it was impossible for me to be anonymous. I didn't know whether it was Brigid's intentional spreading of the news about my circumstances or the student body's natural curiosity over "the new girl," but suddenly, people I had never met before were greeting me in the halls and saving me seats in class.

"Ya should be glad people have taken a likin' ta ya," Declan stated as he walked me to my fifth hour Gaelic class.

"I don't feel liked," I frowned. "I feel scrutinized." I looked behind me, and a group of girls with pigtails and dimples smiled and waved as if to prove my point.

"Come on, Arella. They're just tryin' ta make ya feel welcome." Declan's lips twitched into a sarcastic smile. "Ya're practically a rockstar ta 'em."

"They don't get out much, do they?"

"No, guess not," he laughed.

"When I'm not around to entertain the masses, what keeps things exciting on Tory?"

Declan wrinkled up his forehead as he tried to find an answer to my question. "Well, we don't have many rock concerts on the island, but we do have céilis."

"Céilis?" I wasn't even sure I pronounced it correctly.

"Aye, Irish music and dancin' at Club na Maighdine Mara. Nearly every night. I'll take ya there sometime if ya like."

"As long as you don't expect me to dance or anything."

We stopped outside the classroom where I had to go for instruction in Gaelic. Declan shook his head in exaggerated denial. "Now then, I would never dream of askin' ya ta do anythin' ta draw attention ta yourself."

"Sure," I said rolling my eyes. "See you in an hour."

Gaelic class was actually one of the less cumbersome subjects on my schedule. Declan had explained that the dialect used on Tory was unique to the island but was close to the Gaelic spoken throughout the rest of County Donegal of which Tory was a part. I didn't care about that really. I just liked the way the words rolled off of my tongue, sounding like an ancient language from a time long gone.

I also liked the professor who taught the class. He was a curious little man named Eoin O'Riley. His wild, orange hair and close-clipped beard reminded me of a leprechaun. Even his mannerisms were quick and nimble, more like a little elf than an elderly professor. I half-expected him to show up to class one day in a suit of kelly green with a pot of gold under his arm instead of a textbook.

"Oileán, island." The words flowed over his tongue like honey from a comb.

"Oileán Thoraigh, Tory Island."

"Daoine, islander."

On and on the words sung in my ears, but they fell flat on my tongue. When I spoke the syllables, they sounded rough and guttural. I couldn't help but feel these people must be genetically predisposed to speaking this lyrical language to be able to make it sound so easy and fluent. I finally gave up butchering the beautiful sounds of their island heritage, closed my eyes, and listened to the rest of the class repeat the lilting tones after Professor O'Riley.

It seemed only moments later that the copper bell brought

the class to their feet. I opened my eyes, startled by the sudden sound of the metallic clanging. The other students pushed back their chairs in hasty unison before scrambling to the exit. I slowly followed suit, stacking my books carefully before rising from my seat.

"Miss Cline, ya best be goin'," Professor O'Riley said. He was right next to my desk, his eyes smiling through the creases at their corners.

I looked up, my cheeks warm with embarrassment. "Sorry." I stood quickly, scraping my chair loudly across the floor.

"Are ya enjoyin' your stay on Tory?"

I fidgeted from one foot to the other as I let my hair fall over my eyes. "I…I haven't been able to see much of it yet."

"Ah, when ya're ready, make sure ya explore Leac na Leannán."

"Leac na…?"

"Leac na Leannán. The Wishin' Stone. 'Tis said that a wish be granted ta anyone who succeeds in throwin' three stones, one right after the other, onta it. Or anyone foolhardy enough ta climb up ta its top. Ya look like ya could use a wish or two granted."

My eyebrows rose betraying my disbelief.

"Ah, probably an old wives' tale, I'm sure. Nonetheless, a sight worth seein'." He punctuated his words with a wink, then turned back to his desk and began shuffling through a stack of loose papers.

Declan was waiting for me when I exited the room.

"How is your Gaelic comin' along?"

"Slow, painfully so."

Declan nodded with a smile as he took my books and tucked them under his arm.

"Do you know where the Wishing Stone is?" The words

tumbled out of me before I had a chance to think.

"Why? Has someone been fillin' ya full of fantastic stories?" Declan's tone was cheery, but his eyes darkened.

I smiled, making light of my request. "Oh, Professor O'Riley said it was worth seeing, is all. Is it near the ruins you're going to show me today?"

"No." Declan's answer was sharp and final.

I bit my lip, wishing I hadn't made the request.

Declan was instantly apologetic. "I'm sorry, Arella, but I wanted ta show ya the lighthouse taday instead. It's on the opposite end of the island. There wouldn't be enough time ta explore both. I thought ya'd rather see somethin' more than a pile of old rocks on your first tour of the island with me."

"The lighthouse?" The words sent a shiver through my body. Dad had planned on showing me the lighthouse.

Yes, yes, the lighthouse, El. I'll take ya there.

The sound of my father's voice whispered in my ear. His words were crisp and clear. I felt his breath on my neck. "Dad?"

"Arella?"

I blinked when I realized Declan was staring at me. I cleared my throat, trying to recover. "My father was planning on showing me the lighthouse before…"

Declan's eyes focused on mine. I felt like a deer caught in the headlights. I fought to tear my gaze away from his, but I couldn't move. "Arella, if ya rather, I could show ya somethin' else."

"No!" The urgency of my voice made Declan blink. I quickly looked away. "I'd like to see the lighthouse. Please take me there."

"Sure, yeah," Declan took my hand. My palm felt clammy against his cool skin. "Tell ya what; we'll make a picnic of it."

"What if it rains?"

"Then we'll get wet." He chuckled, dispelling the eerie

feeling left by the memory of my father's voice.

My last two classes passed quickly. I deliberately immersed myself in the class discussions in the hopes of distracting myself. When the day's final chime of the copper bell rang from its precarious perch atop the tower, I raced from my seat without delay. I didn't see Declan, so I decided to wait against the wall while he made his way through the rush of students flooding the main hallway. Brigid waved as she passed but didn't stop to chat. I was glad she was in a hurry to leave.

"Aye, Arella!"

I turned to see Colin's smiling face coming toward me. "Hi, Colin."

"What're ya doin' standin' 'gainst the wall?"

"Oh, I'm waiting for Declan. Have you seen him?"

"Not since theology. Is he s'posed ta meet ya here?"

"Yeah, we were going to walk home together, then go out to the lighthouse."

"Is that right?" His red eyebrows knitted together into a scarlet unibrow.

"Yeah, would you like to come along?"

His pensive brows rose and separated once again. "Yeah, sounds good."

"What does?" Declan's voice cut through the hallway chatter.

"Oh, Colin wants to come with us to the lighthouse."

Declan playfully punched Colin's shoulder. "I thought ya said the lighthouse was dull, Donland?"

"What?" Colin's confused face suddenly flashed understanding. "Oh, I see. It's a private tour, then. Don't ya be worryin' 'bout me. I'll just sit home by myself. Get ahead on my studies or clean my room. That'll be more interestin' anyway."

"That sounds productive." Declan slapped Colin on the back, dismissing him before taking my books.

"Declan!" I looked at him with angry eyes. "Colin, you can come too." I took back my books to show Declan I wouldn't be deterred.

"Naw, I've been ta the lighthouse a hundred times," Colin replied.

"Then you can help give me the tour."

My insistence made him look to Declan for approval.

I continued, "We'll make it a picnic. I'll make the sandwiches."

Declan sighed but took back my books anyway. "Your timin' is first rate, Donland. Meet us at the lighthouse in one hour then."

"Right. Bye, Arella." Colin zipped away through the crowd of students streaming out of the school.

Declan tried to make conversation with me on the way home from school, but I was still a little mad at him for trying to exclude Colin. He finally gave up. We walked in silence past a few houses until we were standing in front of his red and orange cottage. He paused for a moment then said, "I'll meet ya at your house at half past three. I have ta change my clothes and pack some food." He handed me my books.

"All right." I smiled.

Declan winked then trotted up the dirt path to his front door.

When I got back to Aunt Fi's cottage, I found her sitting at her easel, brush in hand, an intent look on her face.

"What are you painting?"

"Oh, Arella, dear," she said, her face suddenly animated. "I'm workin' on your picture. What do ya think?"

I walked to where she was working and gazed over her shoulder. The canvas was awash in color. Deep blues, vibrant greens, warm browns, and balmy oranges flowed forth from the painting, filling my eyes with a surreal perspective of my aunt's view of her island home. "Is that Tory's lighthouse?"

"'Tis, lass."

"It's…" For a moment, I couldn't find words enough to describe it. "It's absolutely phenomenal! Where did you learn to paint like that?"

"Oh, I never learned ta paint. Ya don't learn ta do somethin' that just flows from ya naturally, now. Ya got ta just let how ya feel control what ya do." She ended her sentence with a wink.

I nodded dumbly. Though I wasn't quite sure, it seemed like there was a double meaning to her words.

"Well, it not be done yet, but I'm glad ya approve."

"Declan is taking me to the lighthouse today. We're going to have a picnic with Colin Donland there. I can't wait now to see what it looks like in person."

"Be sure an' wear a sweater so ya don't be catchin' a chill."

"I will." I hurried to my room. I dropped my books on my bed and wiggled out of my stiff uniform, leaving it crumpled on the floor where it dropped. I slipped into a pair of jeans and a t-shirt and grabbed a navy blue sweatshirt as promised.

I went to the kitchen and began rummaging through my aunt's ice box. It looked more like a piece of antique furniture than an appliance. Its white paint was chipped and yellowed. The door to the ice drawer was permanently soiled with at least sixty or seventy years' worth of fingerprints. The hardware was dark with tarnish. I shook my head, not understanding why my aunt refused to modernize her life. I looked inside for some lunchmeat but settled on making cheese and mustard sandwiches when the only meat I found was some fatty looking gray loafs wrapped in wax paper.

I went to the oak cabinet my aunt used as a pantry and

rummaged through it to see what I could find. I opened a round, tin box. It was full of hard, biscuit-like cookies. I tasted one. A little plain, but it would go down well with milk. "Aunt Fi, do you have a thermos I could borrow to put some milk in," I called into the other room.

"No, dear, but ya can take a bottle with ya."

I went back to the ice box. There were three bottles of fresh milk on the top shelf. One was only half-full, so I took that one. The weather outside was cool. I figured the milk would stay fresh until we drank it.

I gathered up my little hoard of snacks and carried them to the front room. Aunt Fi was still working on my watercolor when I heard a light knock on the mudroom door. I waved to Declan, and he let himself in.

"Declan McQuilan, how are ya now?" Aunt Fi got up from her easel.

"Fine, Miss Cline. And are ya well?"

"Fine, fine. Arella says ya be goin' ta the lighthouse."

"Aye, thought she might like ta see some of our island highlights."

"It's nice of ya ta be so courteous ta my niece, makin' her feel at home on Tory the way ya are."

"Yes, ma'am." Declan looked at me and flashed a crooked smile. "Though she doesn't want ta admit it, I think she's taken a likin' ta our island."

"It's the people that make it special. They make it so ya would never want ta leave." Then as if it were an afterthought, she added, "Leaving is never a choice."

I stopped myself from rolling my eyes, but I couldn't keep myself from wondering if my aunt had hit her head when she was young to make her just slightly off balance. I might be temporarily stuck here, but I was only one year from legal adulthood. There was no way I would end up spending the rest of my life on this tiny rock.

I broke the awkward silence. "Well, we better get going. Colin will be waiting. See you later, Aunt Fi." I put the sandwiches, snacks, and milk in the wicker basket Declan was holding and quickly ushered him outside.

There were clouds above, but a touch of blue peaked out from behind them. Maybe we would get lucky and have an afternoon free of rain.

"How long of a walk to the lighthouse?" I asked, aware of the possibility the weather could turn on us without notice.

"Oh, not far. Maybe a kilometer."

Once we left the shacks and cottages of West Town behind us, I could see the silhouette of Tory Lighthouse looming in the distance. "So what's the story on the lighthouse?" I asked.

"No story really. I know it was built in the early 1800's. There used ta be a lighthouse keeper, but it's automated now."

"What? No tales to go along with the bricks and mortar? No stories of sailors or light keepers past?" I coaxed, a teasing smile on my face.

Declan laughed, "No, sorry, nothin' that excitin', I'm afraid. There was an ancient tomb once in East Town. It's gone now, but they say the stones were used ta build the lighthouse walls. But there aren't any ghost stories of wrecked sailors or trapped souls refusin' ta leave their former life's residence, if that's what ya mean. The dead are just dead."

My smile melted, and I bit my lip. I walked myself right into that one. I knew it was too late to recover, but I tried anyway, hiding beneath my hair the sober expression creeping over my face.

Declan stammered, "I'm so sorry, Arella. I didn't intend ta…"

"No." I forced myself to smile and look at him. His green eyes were wide with regret. It was obvious he was devastated by the fact that his innocent words had hurt me. "Don't worry about it. I've just... There's been..."

Declan stopped walking and waited for me to finish my thought, but I couldn't. My mind was a jumble of memories, emotions, and fears. I couldn't tell him about the voices and shadows that only I seemed to perceive. How could I explain to Declan, who was trying so hard to make me feel welcome, that his efforts were being wasted on a total nut-job?

"Arella, please talk ta me." Declan's face was an amalgam of concern and frustration.

"I..." Could I trust him with such a secret? "Um...I just remembered that I forgot glasses for the milk I brought." I relied on my old evasion tactic--when stuck in a corner, change the subject.

Declan continued to survey my face. His eyes converged on mine. I felt a disquieting flash of heat under his stare. It started in the pit of my stomach, traveled up my spine, and ended at my cheeks, flooding my face with an uncomfortable surge of warmth. I felt awkward and exposed, with nowhere to hide. I let my hair cover my face again, a poor attempt at avoidance.

"Come on, I want ta show ya somethin'." Declan grabbed my hand and started jogging off the road angling away from the lighthouse. The ground was rocky and uneven. I tripped a few times but used Declan's hand to keep from falling. His fingers were chilly in mine. After a few minutes, we were at the edge of the water looking into a vast wash of blue and gray. There was nothing but sky and ocean in front of me, and there was no line dividing one from the other.

Declan put the basket of food down on the stones and pointed to the left. "See that rock there?"

My eyes followed the direction of his arm. A few meters away, among the shore's pebbles, was a large gray rock. Algae and moss covered the slab of limestone, but anyone could see that it was unusually angular for a natural stone. "What is it?"

"That is Cloch Arclai, the pedestal of the Cursin' Stone."

"Wishing Stone, Cursing Stone-- how many special stones does this island have?"

My question made Declan smile, but he continued his original story without answering me. "Only Cloch Arclai remains, but it is a reminder ta all of the islanders of Tory's mystical past."

I grinned at Declan's words. He was trying to distract me from my somber mood, and I had to admit it was working.

He lowered his voice to a whisper. "Some say that the Cursin' Stone or Cloch na Mallacht was put here by St. Colm Cille. Others say that druids brought the stone ta Tory ta use against their enemies. Regardless of how it got here, it brought with it great magic.

"It was used as part of a pilgrimage called An Turas Mór. The pilgrims would walk the circumference of the island before sunrise, stoppin' at designated points ta place a small stone and say a prayer or curse, as the case may be. Upon returnin' ta Cloch Arclai, they would turn the Cursin' Stone upside down ta end the ritual."

"Where is the Cursing Stone now?" Though the account was obviously just a local folktale, Declan's story telling skills had me wanting more.

"No one knows for sure. The last time anyone saw it was on the eve of September 23, 1884, right before the HMS WASP was dashed upon the rocks just off shore from the lighthouse."

I twisted my chin in skepticism. "You're saying someone deliberately used the Cursing Stone to make the HMS WASP wreck? Why?"

"It was coming ta our island ta collect taxes. The islanders were very poor and desperate. They would have been willin' ta try anythin' ta survive."

"So why hide the Cursing Stone?"

"It isn't known where the stone went. Someone could have taken it, or maybe the sea claimed it. Regardless, it's gone, never ta be used again."

I looked at Declan's face trying to decide if he believed his own tale. His features were smooth, betraying no hint of a lie. "If someone did take it, what good would it do?"

"No more curses could be made, and no curses made could be undone." The corners of Declan's mouth hinted at a smile.

I stood frozen for a moment, thinking about the story. Did he seriously believe this stuff? Just as I was about to question him further, he let out a loud breath and burst out laughing. I punched his shoulder. "Fine, you got me. I was very close to asking to see where the sailors were buried."

Declan stopped laughing, "Oh, the shipwreck is true enough. The graves of the eight crewmen are on the other side of the lighthouse, but as for the story of the Cursin' Stone, well, that I'm sure is a lot of rubbish. Good story though, don't ya think?"

"You're lucky the Cursing Stone isn't here now, Declan McQuilan, or you'd be begging me for mercy." I emphasized my words by lunging at him with the full intent of knocking him flat on his bottom.

Declan easily evaded my attack, running backward faster than I could run forward. Concentrating on getting my revenge, I didn't see the basket of food lying in my path. Declan easily skirted around it, but I caught my foot on it. I lost my balance and fell forward. The ground rushed up to meet me. There was no time to react other than closing my eyes. I waited for the sharp pain of rough stone crushing into my skin...but it didn't come. I cautiously peeked out from beneath my tightly clenched eyelids. The beach stones were a magnified blur.

"Arella, are ya all right?" Declan asked as he helped me to my knees.

"I think so. Am I bleeding?" My fingers instinctively searched my face for signs of an injury. Funny, I felt my face hit the rocks, but there wasn't any pain.

"No, not a scratch on ya." Declan ran the back of his hand along the length of my right cheek, his skin cold against my face. His eyes moved slowly, back and forth, analyzing my features. Gently, his fingers traced their way to my right temple. His touch was careful, but I flinched away from its chill. He ran a finger along my scar, and his eyes darkened. Was it sadness or pity? I couldn't tell.

I pulled away, burying all recollections of the accident before they could fester to awareness. I ducked my head to let my hair cover the horrible mark which branded me a sympathy case to everyone around me. I had to escape this memory of pain breaking through my thin façade of indifference. I pushed Declan's hand away, not intentionally but as a protective reflex. "I'm fine now. We should find Colin."

"El, I know this must be hard for ya, but I am your friend. I want ta help."

"For starters, don't call me El." My voice was a mixture of irritation and sadness. I didn't know how I should feel about Declan trying so hard to be nice, and my jumble of emotions was coming out as pure anger. "And second, don't touch my face."

Declan leaned back on his heels. "All right." The bit of light peeking through the clouds shone down on his face, tinting his green eyes slightly blue. "I'll do my best ta comply, but if I should forget, ya won't hesitate to remind me, will ya? Nicely though, I'm a wee bit sensitive when it comes ta such things."

I looked at his face, trying to decipher the feeling behind the words. For a moment, I thought that he was serious, but then the corners of his mouth twitched, and I couldn't help but smile at my absurdly defensive behavior. "Sorry. Truce?"

Declan stood and offered me his hand. "Sure, a truce. However, I have some demands of my own now. If we're ta be friends, it has ta go both ways."

I cocked my head to the side unsure if I was walking into a trap. "All right. State your demands."

"First, when somethin' is botherin' ya, tell me before it turns ta anger. And second, stop worryin' 'bout Colin. Ya'll only encourage him."

Encourage him? Encourage him to do what? I was about to verbalize the questions darting around in my head when I heard Colin's familiar voice calling.

Chapter Five

There ya are. I was lookin' for ya all around the lighthouse," Colin exclaimed, his freckled cheeks puffing heavy breaths.

"Hi, Colin. Declan was showing me the Cloch Ar…"

"Cloch Arclai." Colin finished the Gaelic term before I had a chance to butcher it.

"Right. And telling me about the Cursing Stone."

"Was he now?" Colin's bushy, red eyebrows rose high on his forehead. "What other island secrets has he divulged?"

Declan frowned at Colin and shook his head slightly. Then he quickly said, "Come on then; I'm starvin'. Let's pick a spot at the base of the lighthouse where we can eat a bit."

"Right." Colin didn't need to be coaxed. He grabbed the basket of food and hurried along in the direction of Tory Lighthouse.

Declan grabbed my hand and led me after him, his icy touch sending an excited chill up the length of my arm.

"Declan, what other secrets is Colin talking about?" I asked, closely studying his face.

Declan shook his head before answering and slowed our pace. "Pay no attention ta Colin. He lives with his grandmother, and she fills him full of island stories."

"What kind of stories?" I pressed.

Declan frowned. His hand squeezed my fingers tighter. "Arella, we Irish are full of stories and tales of the past. We speak of curses and magic and secrets because it's a part of who we are. We're a story tellin' people, but our tales are not the truth. Oh, the stories started out as the truth in the beginnin', but over the centuries, every storyteller has embellished, changed, and enhanced the tales until there's but an ounce of truth left in each account."

"I know that your folktales aren't your true history, but why are you so concerned that Colin believes a little more in the stories than most?"

"Not just Colin, but most of the villagers will tell ya fantastic tales and island secrets, swearin' they're true." Declan stopped to laugh. "Now do not think badly of them; they're just proud of the only thing of value ta them…their heritage."

I dropped Declan's hand and stopped walking. Declan turned to look at me. His eyes were dark, and his jaw was clenched.

"Declan, I'm sorry if I gave you the idea that I looked down on the islanders. I don't, not at all. I…I just know that I'm not one of them. I don't fit in."

"Ya weren't one of us, but ya are now." Declan smiled as he took my hand back and cradled my palm in his. "I just don't want ya ta be thinkin' that Tory is full of a lot of superstitious rubes. Or think that I'm like that."

I shook my head. "No, I wish I could claim a share in your history."

"Ya can! It's your heritage, too, ya know."

I smiled, but I knew Declan's words were false. My father may have gone to school on Tory, and my aunt may still live on the island, but I had no claim to it.

We walked along the rocky shore toward the lighthouse. The gray surf beat the shoreline in a slow, sad rhythm. Grass tufts, growing between the crags of limestone, waved in the breeze. The wind whipped my hair across my face, making my eyes tear. I wiped the back of my hand across my cheek, smearing the moisture into my skin.

"Come on, now," Colin called from a few hundred feet

ahead.

"Go on then. We'll catch up in a bit," Declan answered.

Colin huffed off, shaking his head.

In the distance, the silhouette of a large ship buoyed against the horizon. The wind shifted direction, and the overpowering smell of salt and fish assaulted my senses. A lone sea bird complained from above as the clouds began to swirl. The sun, which had made a brief appearance at the start of our outing, was now obscured.

Tory Lighthouse stood out against the sky's gray backdrop. The light tower was a bold black and white stripe, a beacon to both land and sea. Its outbuildings were less pronounced, alternating white and gray exteriors. A low brick and mortar wall ran around the entire complex, making it look like its own little hamlet.

"What are those buildings around the light?"

"One was the keeper's residence. That one with the shakes." Declan pointed to the largest of the structures. It had three chimneys making it look like an oversized cottage. "The others were various outbuildings. They're all used for storage now."

"Even the house?"

"No, the house is rented out ta tourists now and again."

"Hey, takin' your good ol' time, are ya?" Colin called from the steps outside the light.

"Unlike ya, Colin, I was bein' polite, lettin' Arella take in the scenery."

"Well, I'm starvin'. I could eat a whale if it washed up on shore right now."

"I don't doubt ya could," Declan agreed with a smirk.

"Don't worry; I made plenty of sandwiches," I assured them. "I hope you like cheese and mustard."

Colin smiled wide. "It's not pickle loaf, but it'll do."

I laughed aloud. "I was wondering what that gray stuff in wax paper was. You actually eat that stuff?"

"Oh, yea. It's really tasty with relish."
I held back my sudden urge to gag and just nodded politely.

Declan saw my face and chuckled. Then he spread out a blanket at the base of the light. Colin sprawled out on it, making himself comfortable.

"Sandwiches with cookies and milk, not much of a meal, I'm afraid," I said as I handed out everyone's portion.

Declan volunteered, "Well, I brought a few apples and pears. That should make it a bit more filling."

"Any sardines?" Colin asked, his mouth already full with a bite of his cheese sandwich.

"Sorry, fresh out," Declan said, rolling his eyes.

Colin shook his head. "What kind of picnic is this? No pickle loaf and no sardines? Next time, I'm packin' the food."

"Next time, don't invite yourself."

"I didn't. Arella did," Colin protested.

Both boys turned to me, obviously waiting for me to take sides. I took a bite of my sandwich and ducked my gaze so I was safe behind my bangs. Let them duke it out; I was staying out of this one. I chewed my brown bread sandwich in silence, refusing to be sucked into their game.

"Well, what should I show ya after we eat?" Declan asked after a few moments of awkward silence.

"Can we go up in the light?" I asked, my interest suddenly piqued, forgetting the silent treatment I was trying to lay on them.

Declan's smile was back. "Sure we can."

"Do we need to purchase tickets somewhere or get a guide?"

Colin and Declan looked at each other in silence. Colin's eyes blinked once. His right eyebrow rose slightly, asking a silent question.

Declan's jaw twisted to the left. His lips pressed together in a hard, thin line. "No," he answered, "Everyone on Tory knows everyone else. As long as we don't harm anythin', no one will mind."

"If you're sure." I wasn't, but I didn't know what the silent exchange meant, so I would just have to trust that we wouldn't get into trouble. Besides, if we did, maybe that would be my ticket off this foggy rock.

We packed away the remains of dinner and left the basket sitting on the limestone steps to be retrieved after our sightseeing expedition. Declan went to the whitewashed door of the light tower, twisted the knob, and gestured me forward with a smile and a wave. I crossed my arms over my chest and forced myself toward the gloom spilling through the doorway. Colin fell in line right behind me like he was making sure I couldn't back out.

"Maybe we shouldn't. I mean, it's private property, and it's dark. We might fall." I instinctively raised my hand to the scar on my temple. I rubbed it, trying to ease the imaginary ache.

"Come on, Arella. The view is worth the climb." Declan took my hand away from my temple and gently laced his fingers through mine. He flashed me his gap-toothed grin before disappearing inside the doorway.

Sigh. "OK, you only live once. Might as well live on the edge, right?" I reluctantly followed him into the tower's dark interior. The air was musty. I felt my pupils immediately stretch wide, gathering the bit of light that entered through the dirty windows far above us. A loud bang sounded behind me. I turned abruptly, squeezing Declan's fingers tighter.

"It's OK, Arella," Declan's voice echoed in the darkness as he pried my fingernails from where they were embedded in his skin. "Colin just closed the door."

"Why? Shouldn't we leave it open so we can find our way out?" My voice was shaky despite my attempt at casual indifference.

Colin's voice cut through the black air, "'Tis best if we put everythin' back the way it should be. Don't want ta cause unnecessary worry."

"We're not supposed to be here, are we? Let's go. I don't need a tour." I started pulling Declan in the direction where I thought the door should be, but the darkness was too disorienting for me to be sure.

Declan's voice was a calm whisper. "Just trust me, Arella. It'll be all right. No one minds our comin' here as long as we don't disturb anythin'." He tucked my arm through his and led me forward. "Watch your step. Just hold on ta me in case ya miss a step. There are ninety-four all tagether."

My shins hit the front of the first step. Reluctantly I raised my foot and started to climb. One, two. The staircase spiraled around and around. Nine, ten. Our feet clanged on the metal steps and echoed through the dark, empty tower. Fourteen, Fifteen. Higher and higher we climbed. Twenty-one, twenty-two. The stairs kept spiraling. Thirty-seven, thirty-eight. I heard my own breath coming faster, but I couldn't figure out whether it was the climb or my nerves pushing me towards hyperventilation. Fifty-three. Why did I agree to this? My heart pounded wildly, and my pulse roared in my ears. From above, a dim light seeped down into the darkness. Seventy-nine. We were either gonna break our necks or be tossed in jail. That last option almost cheered me up. I didn't think Tory had a jail; maybe they would send us to the mainland for incarceration. Ninety-two, ninety-three, ninety-four. Thank God!

I let out my breath in a loud puff and hung my chin to my knees. I squeezed Declan's fingers. Mine were icy and stiff with fear. His were just as cold, but I doubted if it was for the same reason.

Colin's voice filled the silence. "Wasn't so bad now, was it?"

"I'll let you know once I can breathe again."

"Come see the view, Arella." Declan pulled me along the metal platform toward the dim light filtering through the grimy lighthouse windows.

Hesitantly, I shuffled my lead feet after him. I could feel my pupils contracting away from the growing brightness. I heard the click of a latch as Declan opened a heavy metal door leading out to a catwalk. A gust of ocean breeze whooshed through the doorway. The heavy hatch swung wide, groaning against the force. We stepped out onto the metal walkway into the fresh island air.

Colin sucked in a deep, loud breath of air. "Smells a might bit fresher out here, it does." He stretched out his arms over his head as he puffed out his chest, cleansing his lungs of the lighthouse's stale odor.

My eyes finished adjusting to the brightness as I took in the panorama stretching out around me. The ocean reached out in front of me, ebbing toward the horizon in gray and navy waves. Where the sea and sky met, there was no division. One merged into the other like two fluids converging in a vast basin. My eyes scanned the craggy shoreline. The rocks were a collage of grays and browns, edged in moss. From this vantage point, the island and the sea surrounding it looked like the setting from an Irish fairytale, vivid but unchanging. "It's fantastic!" I breathed. Here was a place of myth and magic, not a desolate place of internment.

Declan placed his hand on the small of my back. "Have ya ever seen such a sight?"

I shook my head. I was at a loss for words. How could I verbalize the fact that for me it could never be the people that held me bound to this island, but rather what the people could not touch or change? If ever I could be made to dwell in this place, it would be because of the island's rough resistance against the harsh forces that made it beautiful and drew me in.

Declan smiled triumphantly, "Ya see now, Tory has a way of charmin' everyone, even the most stubborn."

The corners of my mouth curled up, but I didn't allow myself to smile. Two people walking below caught my attention. It was a woman and a little girl. The woman had long, dark hair that tangled behind her in the breeze. The little girl looked to be seven or eight. Her hair was blond and pulled back in a messy ponytail. They were walking along the rocks, pausing here and there, bending down to examine random bits of stone that caught their attention. When the little girl looked up at the lighthouse, I waved automatically.

Declan swiftly grabbed my hand. "Ya shouldn't draw attention ta us."

"Why not?"

Declan's eyes darted back and forth across my face. "We'll have a whole crowd up here if ya let on that people can climb ta the top, don't ya know."

"Oh, sure." I looked back to the little girl and the woman. The woman was still busy peering intently at the ground, but the little girl was standing still, looking up at us. I resisted the urge to wave. I smiled but doubted that she saw.

The wind changed direction, blowing my hair in my face. I closed my eyes instinctively. A strange array of colors danced behind my lids. The sun...only, there was no sun. I slowly opened my eyes to look at the people below. The little girl was still staring up at us. Declan and Colin stood perfectly still, ignoring her scrutiny. I blinked. The bright colors were still there behind my eyelids. I closed my eyes tightly and studied the light filtering through the skin covering my pupils. Dark green rays surrounded by purple flames. I peeked at the people below. The woman was waving for the little girl to follow, but the child ignored her beckoning. The youngster stood still, gazing up at us. She raised a hand as if to wave, then turned and skipped after the woman who was wandering away from the lighthouse toward Cloch Arclai. I closed my eyes again. The colors and lights were gone, and so were the little girl and her mother.

"Where did they go?"

"Arella?" Declan's voice cut through the sound of the wind. "We best be leavin'."

"Sure." I shook my head, trying to clear the questions beginning to swarm in my brain. "We better get out of here before those people tell someone they saw us."

Colin barked a laugh. "I wouldn't worry 'bout it now. No one'd believe 'em."

I caught Declan shooting Colin a disapproving look. Then his eyes shot to mine, and he smiled. "Don't want your Aunt Fi thinkin' we kidnapped ya now. Best get home before it gets dark."

The sky was only a light gray, but I nodded and let Declan usher me back toward the lighthouse door.

Chapter Six

"Would ya like ta go ta the céili with me tonight?" Declan's smile flickered anxiously as I stood silently trying to remember what a céili was. "That's a dance, right?"

"Right, most of the islanders will be there. They'll be playin' traditional Irish music, but ya'll also get a taste of some of the local songs as well."

"I don't know." I stared down at my scuffed patent leathers. They were finally starting to look broken-in even though they still squished my toes. "I'm not really into Irish music, and I don't like to dance."

"Come on, Arella. Most of our friends will be there. It's a good time. Everyone dances and sings, whether they're good at it or not."

The large copper bell started to clang. "We better hurry or Father Dalbach will have a fit," I said.

Declan grabbed my hand as I tried to hurry toward the courtyard of the Academy. "Not 'til ya say ya'll go."

"I'll think about it."

"Not good enough."

"Maybe."

"Do I have ta beg ya now?" Declan got down on one knee.

I could feel my face flushing with embarrassment as a pair of girls hurried past us, stifling giggles. "No, Declan."

"No, ya won't go, or no I don't have ta beg?"

"Declan!" I looked around to see if anyone else was witnessing his humiliating display. Luckily, all the other students seemed to be on time for their first hour class. It was just the two of us. I looked down to see him exaggerating a pout, while his green eyes glinted with mischief. Argh! He wasn't going to let me off easy. "I'll make you a deal."

"Fair enough."

"I'll go to the dance—or céili—with you, but I don't have to dance or sing. Deal?"

Declan smiled in triumph. "Ya don't have ta do anything ya don't want ta do." He stood quickly and brushed the dust from the knees of his black dress pants.

The copper bell chimed. "Crap, now we're late for theology. I doubt Father Dalbach's going to let us off so easy for this tardy."

"Ah, he'll make us say a few *Hail Mary's* and an *Act of Contrition* at worst."

I rolled my eyes at Declan's indifference. He winked and then pulled me into a run toward the doors of St. Colm's.

We skidded to a stop outside Father Dalbach's classroom. The priest had his back to the door as he passed out packets of papers to the already seated class. Declan put his finger to his lips and pulled me through the door. We slid along the side wall, trying to avoid attracting anyone's attention. Everyone was flipping through the pages of the packet, groaning over Father Dalbach's soon to be assigned project, not seeming to notice our late arrival. Everyone except Colin.

Colin sat slouched in his seat, totally uninterested in the stack of papers sitting on his desk. He leaned back with a loud yawn, stretching his arms to the girl sitting behind him. She smacked the back of his head, making him twist around in self-defense. Declan put his finger to his mouth, and Colin gave him a quick thumbs-up.

"Please turn ta the outline on the first page," Father Dalbach said, starting to turn toward us.

Colin quickly chucked his pen at a chubby boy sitting in the front row. Declan and I ducked into our seats just as a stream of profanities burst from the wounded boy's lips.

Father Dalbach's face turned from red to purple as the boy's words registered. "Master Gallagher, do ya mind tellin' me what evil spirit has suddenly taken possession of your tongue, so's I can exorcise it from ya?"

"Someone hit me head," the boy protested as he rubbed his chunky fingers over an invisible bump on the back of his skull. The classroom echoed with his classmates' chuckles.

"Perhaps 'twas your guardian angel remindin' ya ta pay attention ta your elders." Father Dalbach's beaded eyes scanned our faces, obviously looking for the 'guardian angel.'

"There's no such thing as guardian angels," Gallagher disputed.

The priest pointed an accusing finger toward the boy as his voice lashed out, "Are ya disagreein' with me, now?"

Perspiration dripped down the accused's temples, leaving no doubt of his discomfort. "No, sir," he squeaked.

"I thought not. Now, if ya would, Master Gallagher, stand by your seat and recite the *Act of Contrition* so as ta let Our Lord Jesus Christ know that ya are truly sorry for the foul words ya let escape from the mouth he gave ya."

The boy hesitated for a moment, looking around at the suddenly solemn faces staring at him. He wiped the sweat gathering along his hairline and then hauled himself up from the seat.

"Tuck in your shirt, lad," the priest snapped.

Gallagher pushed his pudgy fingers around his waistband. His face went white, and he looked like he was going to faint. "Oh, My God..." The words came out like an expletive. "I am sorry for my sins..."

I looked at Colin. He was stifling a laugh. My stomach started to churn with guilt. Gallagher looked like he was about to faint.

"I have sinned, sinned, sinned," he stuttered on.

I couldn't take it. My hand flew up. Both Father Dalbach and Gallagher looked at me in surprise.

"Yes, Miss Cline, has Master Gallagher erred in his prayer, or are ya volunteerin' ta join him in his recitation?"

My throat was suddenly dry. "No, no," I stammered. "I just…well, it's not his…"

Declan's voice drowned out the rest of my sentence. "It's not his fault. It's not Gallagher's fault." He stood. "I threw a pen at 'im and hit his head. He was tellin' the truth."

"Well, now." Father Dalbach's small eyes narrowed to slits. "'Tis the second time that ya caused a disturbance in my classroom. I think that ya're long overdue on servin' penance, wouldn't ya say."

I looked at Declan's face. There was no hint of a smile now.

"Yes, Father." His words were solemn.

Father Dalbach put his hands behind his back and puffed out his chest. "Both ya and Master Gallagher will report ta Father Cillian's after last hour today. I'll be makin' sure that he's expectin' ya, so don't be late."

I jumped from my seat, standing in Declan's defense. "It's my fault, Father." I could see Colin from the corner of my eye. He was shaking his head in warning, but I ignored him. "Declan and I were late to class because of me, and we were trying to sneak in unnoticed."

Father Dalbach screwed up his narrow chin in thought. "Miss Cline, I don't know that your aunt would be approvin' of such behavior from her niece. It would be a shame, don't ya know, ta upset her with news of your unladylike behavior."

"Unladylike? What are you talking about?" Instead of feeling guilty, I was now feeling angry.

"Just look at ya! I haven't said anythin' 'bout it 'til now, 'cause I was hopin' ya'd straighten up after awhile, but I think I've let it go on long enough."

I was at a loss. His words held so much venom I couldn't sift through what he was talking about. "I'm sorry. I don't understand," I managed to voice between gritted teeth. This guy was starting to act like he was barely a step below God himself, making me forget that I usually didn't like to attract attention to myself.

"Take your nails, for one. Black is the color of Satan and all his works, yet ya choose ta paint your nails the very color. Did ya not have sufficient time ta read the dress code? And your skirt. Does your aunt know that ya roll it sos the hem is up ta your thigh? What God-fearin' young lady parades around like such a harlot?"

"Father," Declan interrupted, "it's unfair of ya ta judge Arella so harshly. Remember that she's not from Tory."

Father Dalbach slammed his hand down on the student desk directly in front of him. The little blond girl sitting there let out a terrified squeal. "Do not tell me what is unfair. The good Lord gives each of us what we deserve, and Miss Cline is no different. Perhaps he decided that the only way for her ta appreciate the gifts given ta her was ta take 'em away."

The priest's spiteful words burned through me like a red, hot poker. How could someone claiming to be a servant of God say such horrible things? But then, maybe he was right, and maybe that was what really hurt. Maybe God was punishing me for taking my parents for granted. My voice came out as a whisper, but I think everyone in the room heard me say, "You're right. I really don't fit in here, and it was probably foolish of me to try." I looked at the students' blank faces staring back at me. I felt a momentary sense of longing. Actually, in that moment, I wished I did belong. "Thanks anyway," I said, turning toward the door.

The room was silent except for the slow clicking echo of my damned patent leather shoes. Once outside the room, I let my tears fall, blurring my vision. I hurried down the hall toward the heavy doors and heard them bang loudly behind me as I exited the Academy. Their sound punctuated the loud sob that escaped my chest as the damp air hit my lungs. I blew out a wheezy breath and started running toward West Town's pier.

I really didn't know where I would go. I knew Aunt Fi would be devastated, but I couldn't bring myself to stay in a place where I couldn't fit in. I'd somehow have to get back to the States. I could probably steal my way onto the ferry back to Bunbeg or Magheraroarty without anyone noticing, but it would be harder getting from the mainland back to America. I'd cross that bridge or ocean when I came to it, I guessed.

Luckily, the streets of West Town were empty except for an old man carrying a pole over his shoulders, the ends of which held two sloshing buckets of water. Geez, there wasn't even running water to all of the houses. Tory Island really was a flash from the past. I continued to hurry through the middle of town past a t shaped monument: the Tau Cross. Such a rudimentary symbol of the early Christian faith gave further proof of how truly ancient this island was.

I turned the corner and caught sight of the pier. No one was around. Making sure I was hidden in the shadows, I ran close to the edge of an old warehouse. When I was just a hundred feet or so from the pier, I stopped running and took a deep breath to clear my head. I was going through with this. No backing out now. I closed my eyes, blocking out all thoughts of turning around.

Behind my lids, the darkness was soothing. I was thankful I could block out the decrepit buildings and dusty roads surrounding me. I didn't want any memory of this ugly place.

I took another deep breath. This time, I wrinkled my nose.

Even the air reeked of rotting boards and desolation, the same smell that exuded from every antique store my parents had ever forced me to enter, the pungent odor of musty heirlooms and moth-eaten lace.

As I started to open my eyes, I noticed a tiny point of light searing through the blackness behind my eyelids. It was no bigger than a pinhead at first, but it grew steadily. The light's intensity and color flared shades of blue and turquoise. I clenched my eyes tighter, trying to block it out, but it only blazed brighter. In a sudden panic, I flashed my eyes wide, expecting to see the oncoming headlights of a speeding car racing toward me. Instead, I was face to face with Cannon Fidelous.

"Arella Cline, shouldn't you be at the Academy? Not even a month in school and you're cutting class already? Tisk. Tisk. Not the way to win points with your elders."

My stomach churned. Cannon had his arms crossed over his chest. His dark penetrating stare was paralyzing. He smirked like a cat about to pounce a mouse caught in a trap, and I was unable to escape the discomforting awareness of his scrutiny.

A lump swelled in my throat, and I started to sweat, icy beads of moisture forming on the back of my neck and on the palms of my hands. A dry raspy sound escaped from my lungs as I forced myself to steady my breathing. It took all of my will to finally shake off his invisible hold, twist in the opposite direction, and back away.

"Wait a second." He put his hand on my shoulder and spun me back around. "What's your hurry?" His forehead was creased with disappointment. "I just wanted to talk for a minute."

I wasn't in the mood for talking, but I crossed my arms and waited for him to continue.

Cannon's smile returned. It was gloating and full of spite, nothing like Declan's mischievous but benevolent grin. "You don't like this place, do you?"

I shrugged.

"You know you can't leave."

I narrowed my eyes on his nasty smirk, but I remained silent. He was baiting me, and I wasn't about to bite.

"You didn't know that, did you? No matter how hard you try, you can't cross the water." Cannon waited for me to question him. When I didn't, he continued. "It's like an invisible barrier keeping us all here. Hell, you can't even leave in a box."

I shook my head, forcing my hair out of my eyes for once. "All right, what's your story, Cannon? You're the only American here besides me, and you seem to have all the answers." I poked my finger into his chest for emphasis. "So tell me, what is your deal?"

"Oh, my story is the same as yours practically. I ended up on this island by chance, not by choice. Bad luck really. I tried to fit in at the Academy, but I hated it, too many rules and regulations for my taste. After a week, I quit."

"Then why are you still here?" I could taste the ice in my tone, and I hoped Cannon could feel it.

"I told you. There's no way to leave. Not even by..." Cannon sliced his finger across his throat like he was slitting it.

"You're delusional. I'm out of here on the next ferry."

Cannon barked a laugh. "Try it. See how far you'll get."

"What are you talking about? I've got money to pay my way back to Bunbeg, and from there I'll hitch a ride to the airport."

"Do you remember arriving on the ferry?"

"No, not exactly."

"Why not?"

I paused because I didn't want to face the answer to his question. I had tried not to think about anything in the past. I was afraid that the memories of the accident would surface to haunt me. With venom in my voice, I finally responded, "I was still in shock I guess. I've been in a daze ever since my parents... What are you getting at?"

"My point is that you don't just come and go on Tory like you would any other island. I don't remember coming here either, but I'm here just like you. And anytime I've tried to get away, whether by ferry or rowboat or swimming, I've ended up on shore, unconscious and totally oblivious to how I got there. There's no escaping Tory. Believe me, if there was a way, I would have found it."

"You're crazy." I pushed past him heading toward the dock. "You've been in this loony-bin too long. I'm leaving on the next ferry out of here before I end up a nut-case like you."

"Suite yourself," Cannon called after me. "But when you find yourself back on Tory's rocky shore, dazed and confused and unable to remember how you got there, remember that I warned you."

I turned to look back at him. "Why would you bother to warn me?"

Cannon's smile faded. "I think it's too late for me to leave, but maybe you'll get lucky. It's harder for me to remember my old life. I don't remember my father at all, but I keep picturing this woman with long brown hair and green eyes. I think it could be my mom. Can you still remember your family?"

Tears started to well in my eyes as I forced myself to recall my parents' faces. My mother's green eyes flickered in my mind as her full pink lips turned up in a smile, showing her small pearly teeth. I sighed in relief. Yes, I still remembered her, as clear as day. I concentrated on resurrecting my father's features next. I saw his gray hair and round face. I started to nod in reply to Cannon's question, but I stopped in shocked horror as I realized I couldn't picture his eyes. Those eyes that had stared into mine so many times in reassurance and love were now nondescript and strange, dark and lifeless.

"Well, can you?" he demanded.

I felt myself nervously biting my lip. "Of course," I lied.

The ferry's horn pierced through the fog clinging to the air over the bay. My heart jumped in my chest and knocked me back to consciousness. Cannon was trying to give me a line of crap, and I was done listening to it. I turned and hurried toward the ticket window at the end of the dock. I clattered over the warped planks, listening to the empty sound of my black patent leathers, while trying to ignore Cannon's incessant jeers.

"I'll see you tomorrow, Arella. I'm sure you'll be looking for something to do since you won't be returning to the Academy. You can find me at Balor's Fort most days."

The ferry's horn sounded again, and I could just barely make out a ship's faint outline in the fog. In another minute, the vessel was in the harbor. It rocked up next to the dock as two deckhands tossed and fastened ropes. The ramp lowered.

I peered at the old man sitting inside the ticket booth. His chin was on his chest, and he was snoring. "Excuse me, sir. Can I get a ticket back to the mainland, please?"

"Wha, what?" he stuttered, startled out of his sleep. He rubbed his gray eyes until the lids were red. Then he said, "Ya can, don't ya know, but I'll offer no guarantees."

I wondered at his comment but decided I didn't have time for explanations. I handed him a wad of bills from my pocket and grabbed the ticket. After handing it to the crewman standing on the ramp, I anxiously took a spot on deck next to the rail.

I looked back at the pier, afraid Cannon would be trailing me. It was empty. He must have decided he finally lost the game he was playing. Funny, the deck of the ferry was empty too, except for me and two crewmen. My own private boat. Weird. Whatever. As long as I got out of here, I didn't need company or fanfare.

The horn blasted, and with a sudden jerk, the ferry eased out of position and headed back into the fog from where it had emerged. I drummed my fingers on the railing; its white paint was chipped and scraped. Even the ferry to this godforsaken place was in sore need of repair.

A wave splashed up, and a salty spray peppered my face. I licked my lips and closed my eyes. The darkness behind my lids could not squelch the feeling of loss and loneliness I felt in the pit of my stomach. I really hadn't decided on my end destination, but, when I did, I would stay as far away from the sea as possible.

El, come back. My father's voice resonated through the hum of the ferry's engine.

My breath caught in my throat as my eyes opened wide looking for someone I knew could not be there. The fog had become thicker, and it wrapped around me like a shroud. I labored to breathe, but my lungs were stones in my chest. I took a desperate gulp of air, trying to suck oxygen from the vapor closing in around me.

I felt the deck give way under my feet, though I knew it was my center of balance shifting. I was gonna puke. I was really gonna puke. My head started to swim. I realized then that I wasn't going to puke; I was going to pass out. God, no! I got to my knees, not to pray, but to save myself from falling. And honestly, the thought of making a bargain with God did cross my mind in that moment.

El, we're here. Just open your eyes.

"Daddy?" I forced myself to look, but I was engulfed by the murky mist. I couldn't even see the deck.

El, please don't leave us.

Leave *you*? *I* was the one left behind. *I* was the one who had been abandoned on a crappy rock in the middle of the ocean. "Why should I stay?" I screamed into the gray eddy around me. "This wasn't my choice!" Tears trickled down my cheeks before an avalanche of sobs erupted from my chest. I shuddered as I was enveloped by a paralyzing chill. "I just want to go home." It was a hopeless plea, but I made it anyway.

The fog still swirled around me, but something was taking

shape behind the gloom. I stopped crying and watched as a human form materialized; it was nothing more than a shadow, really, but it moved with a familiar gait, a step full of confidence and authority, but without intimidation. The shadow came closer, but it remained obscured and featureless, and I wasn't frightened. I felt oddly relieved.

El, it's not time for ya ta leave. You can't go. If ya go, we'll not be able ta carry on.

"Daddy, please bring me home." My fingers shook as I reached out to the shadow. The air around me became warm. The ice in my fingers began to thaw. The heat traveled up my arm and into my chest. It pulsed through my veins, making my heartbeat race. My lungs relaxed as I released my breath and then everything went black.

Chapter Seven

*C*rek-crek. *Crek-crek.* The sound was faint but annoying. I turned over and covered my head with a pillow. *Crek-crek. Crek-crek.* "Leave me alone," I mumbled.

"El?"

I rolled over again. The pillow thumped to the ground. My eyes were shut, but brown and gray light edged in a sulfurous yellow filtered through my lids.

"El, wake up."

Crek. My lashes flickered, and I opened my eyes. The lights were gone except for the dim glow of a bedside lamp. I blinked as Declan's face came into focus. He ran his hands through his hair, pushing it out of his bloodshot eyes.

"I told you never to call me El," I croaked through dry lips.

Declan's pale face colored as he smiled. "I had ta do somethin' ta fire ya up, now. How long were ya plannin' on sleepin'?"

"What?" My memory snapped back to the ferry. I sat up and looked around the room. There on the wall opposite me was my family picture. Next to it was a watercolor painted in brilliant shades of color. It was a picture of Tory Lighthouse, the sun rising behind it and Cloch Arclai looming to its left. Obviously my attempt at escape had failed.

"Ya had us worried, Arella. When ya ran out of St. Colm, I didn't know where ta look for ya. It was Cannon Fidelous who came ta me sayin' ya were headed toward the Wishin' Stone. I'm surprised that he would even bother ta help anyone."

"What?" I shook my head. "I don't remember going there." I looked down and saw I was still wearing my school uniform.

My white blouse was wrinkled and smudged, and my kneesocks were torn in several places. Oh well, I wouldn't be needing them anymore.

"Well, that's where we found ya. Ya were throwin' stones and screamin' like a banshee, somethin' 'bout shadows."

"I, I…"

Crek-crek.

"What is that annoying sound?" I pushed myself to my feet to find out but instantly sat back down when the room began to tilt.

Declan chuckled. "Oh, it's the funniest thing. We had ta practically drag ya back home, ya were kickin' and screamin' so. Ya tried ta run away, and when ya did, ya flushed a corncrake out of its nest. The thing's been like a mother hen ta ya ever since. It followed us all the way home and seems ta be keepin' vigil outside your window."

Crek-crek.

I stood up again, more slowly this time, careful not to lose my balance. I padded across the floorboards, put up the shade, and opened the window.

Crek-crek.

Sure enough, in the weeds below, a brown speckled bird the size of a hen was nestled on a bed of dried grass. It looked like a feral chicken.

"The oddest thing is," Declan continued, "corncrakes are extremely shy and rare. I've lived here all my life, and this is the first I've ever seen one. And they're not supposed to be here this time of year either. It's October, and they migrate south in September. Maybe it's your guardian angel, Arella." He smirked slyly. "Maybe ya're blessed."

"More likely cursed." I shut the window with a bang. I sat down on the bed and stared at Declan. His eyebrows rose. "I think…no, I know I'm losing my mind. Nothing is making sense anymore." My voice caught in my throat, and I hung my head to hide my wet eyes.

Declan grabbed my hands, caressing them with his thumbs. "Arella, maybe ya should just accept things instead of tryin' ta figure them out. Just let yourself be happy instead of rejectin' every good thing that comes your way."

He took my chin in his hand. My skin felt like fire against his cool fingers. He raised my head so that I was looking directly into his eyes, emerald irises flecked with gold like polished pebbles in a sea of green. I'd never noticed how brilliant they were. I could get lost in those eyes. It sounded cliché, I know, but it was true. They were like magnets, pulling me in.

His fingers moved slowly to my temple. He ran his thumb along the silvery scar there, but this time, I didn't flinch. I wanted to be angry, but my words came out in a resigned whisper. "I thought I told you not to touch my face. Please."

"I forgot," he murmured as he leaned closer to me.

His lips brushed my cheek, sending ripples of pleasure across my skin. I felt the heat of a blush coloring my face.

"Should I stop?"

I was barely able to whisper. "No." I closed my eyes. The dim light of the nightstand glowed softly behind my lids. Soothing warmth washed over me. It was a brief glimpse of happiness; then, something changed.

Brown and gray lights steadily began to burn through the soft glow, surrounding my bliss with a heavy blanket of doubt. Their intensity slowly grew until I felt like a fugitive caught in a murky spotlight. I gasped for breath and threw open my eyes.

Declan pulled away. "Arella...El, it's all right now. Ya're safe at home."

Home? This wasn't really home. I wanted it to be, but...

Declan slowly moved his hand back to my cheek. He stroked my skin like he was soothing a frightened bird caught in a snare. He leaned in, and I could feel his breath on my face. It sent a delicious shiver through my core. I sighed and let my eyes close.

I felt his mouth move to mine, and for a brief moment, I forgot all the pain and worry that had built up inside of me. Pink lights flared, but I didn't shy away. His lips were warm and gentle, not demanding; when he pulled away, I was left wanting more. I opened my eyes and the lights were gone.

Declan smiled, and I couldn't help but smile back.

Someone cleared their throat in the doorway. "Arella, it's good that ya're awake, lass. And Declan McQuilan, I do believe ya should be excusin' yourself for supper." Aunt Fi's hands were on her hips in a gesture of anger, but her smirk betrayed her amusement.

I bit my top lip and let my bangs cover my blushing face.

"Ya're right, Miss Cline, I should be goin'." Declan squeezed my hand. "And I'll see ya in the mornin', El."

"Declan," I called as he rose from his seat. He paused and I continued. "I won't be going back to the Academy. I've decided it's not for me."

"Ya can't drop out of school. This is your last year before ya graduate." His face was pinched with concern.

My stomach felt queasy, and I could feel the perspiration beading up on my forehead. "I'll get my GED online or something. I just can't go back and face Father Dalbach and the other students after what he said."

Aunt Fi broke in, "Lass, Father Cillian is here ta see ya. He'll make things right, don't ya know." Her eyes were soft with understanding.

"No!" I shook my head back and forth violently. "I'm not going back, Aunt Fi."

"Now, now, Arella, dear, don't be that way. It's only been a few weeks. Give it a bit more time. I'm sure things will improve."

I fell back on my bed exasperated. The room got very quiet. I closed my eyes and sighed. What was the point of returning? Nothing I could learn at St. Colm could help me deal with real life. For instance, what was the purpose of learning Gaelic? Unless I needed to converse with a leprechaun, I doubted I would ever speak a word learned in Professor O'Riley's class. And why did I have to learn the history of Tory Island? Who really cared that the first settlers of Tory were Nemedians from Scythia in Turkey? And theology? Why learn to recite the Fruits of the Holy Spirit? Did it make me a better person if I could rattle them off without thinking twice?

"Ya know, Arella, quittin' was never somethin' your father was fond of." The voice coming from my doorway was unfamiliar.

I sat up to find Aunt Fi and Declan had left the room, and a man with feathery, white hair stood just outside my door. He was short, shorter than any adult I'd ever met, and round. Had he been wearing white instead of the black vestments of a priest, he would have looked like a snowman. His face, however, was bright red, the telltale sign of someone who enjoyed the sacramental wine as much as the sacrament itself. His hands were folded across his fleshy trunk with fingers interlinked like Vienna Sausages in a tin. He rocked back and forth on his heels, looking like a punching clown swaying under someone's blow.

I caught myself staring.

The pudgy cleric continued, "'Twould be an absolute shame, don't ya know, ta miss the opportunity ta learn where your father had come from. If nothin' else, I thought ya would enjoy the prospect of beatin' his record."

"You knew my father?"

"I did indeed. I'm Father Cillian. Pleased ta finally make your aquaintance."

"It's kind of you to come by, but I'm finished with St. Colm's and anything else having to do with this island. I don't belong here." I made my voice as absolute as possible. Then added as an afterthought, "What record are you talking about?"

Father Cillian smiled. He laid a fat finger on his chin and nodded. "Didn't he tell ya that he held St. Colm's record for uniform violations?"

The priest's face was serious. I stared back at him, confused as well as amused at the prospect of my father, Mr. Straight-laced Rule-follower, violating anything. "Those types of things never came up in our father-daughter conversations. Now, if you want to know the ins and outs of the breaching of the walls of Jericho, I can fill you in."

Father Cillian nodded, a thin smile surfacing on his pale lips. "Ya shouldn't be angry with your parents, Arella. They loved ya and did the best they knew how. They were good people."

"I'm not angry with them. I'm angry that I'm stuck here. Why can't I leave?"

"Where would ya go?"

"Home."

"Home is not a place; it's a feelin'."

"Well, I don't get that warm, homey feeling here." I stuck my chin out, crossed my arms over my chest, and waited for the priest to counter.

"Tell ya what. I'm willin' ta let ya drop out of formal classes at St. Colms, if ya'll let me tutor ya instead. We can meet each day durin' school hours, so your schedule would be no different."

I was shaking my head before he finished explaining his proposition. "No, thanks."

"Give me two weeks. If ya still want ta leave then, I'll make the arrangements myself." The odd, little cleric was smirking like he knew he had me. "Arella, ya won't be able ta leave without the Knowledge."

"The Knowledge?" I hated to admit it, but he had my attention.

"Let's just say that I know things that most do not. Things that may be of interest ta ya."

"The only knowledge I'm interested in is how to get out of

here."

The priest narrowed his gaze. "I know."

Something mysterious and possibly sinister was preventing my departure from Tory, and Father Cillian knew it. I had no other choice, so I reluctantly nodded agreement.

Father Cillian grinned, exposing yellowed dentures. "Good, meet me at my door tamorrow mornin', eight o'clock sharp, and we'll begin your lessons. Be sure ta bring your history book." He scuttled out of my room murmuring incoherently about the Knowledge and merit.

Could things really get any more messed up? The entire island and the creatures inhabiting it had me totally weirded-out. Crimony! From the Academy's pastor right down to the corncrakes, Tory Island was an absolute cuckoo's nest.

✝ ✝ ✝ ✝ ✝

I wasn't sure if I should dress in my school uniform for my first class with Father Cillian. I decided to wear my plaid skirt and white blouse. I wasn't, however, in the mood for my toes getting jammed, so I substituted a pair of comfortable running shoes for my black patent leathers. The tennis shoes I chose were silver with yellow trim and clashed with the St. Colm's plaid rather nicely. After lacing them up, I looked in the mirror to admire my motley ensemble and felt an evil sense of satisfaction at my breach of conformity.

What had I to lose? I had already dropped-out of the Academy; the next step would be deportation, and that would be fine by me. I freed the tail of my shirt from my waistband, painted my eyelashes with one more layer of mascara, and grabbed my history book from its place of dishonor under my bed. Kissing Aunt Fi on the cheek, I hurried out the door.

"Arella, ya've changed your mind then," Declan called as I shut the cottage door behind me. He was standing in the middle of the dirt road, his signature gap-toothed grin dancing across his face.

"Well, not exactly." I had forgotten about Declan. "Father Cillian has offered to tutor me."

Declan's features fell. "Won't ya be comin' ta class then?"

I shook my head. "I told you I was done with the Academy. Hopefully, my time with Father Cillian will count as credit toward graduation. And if not…" I shrugged. I wasn't sure what would happen if not.

"Where are ya ta meet him?"

"Outside his office."

"I'll walk ya there."

I smiled, gladly accepting Declan's offer. I knew he was upset about my quitting St. Colm's. Walking to the Academy together would make both of us feel a little better about the current situation.

We entered St. Colm's main doors just as the first bell began to clang. Declan tried to ignore its warning of tardiness, but I insisted he not be late on my account. "I know the way to Father Cillian's office. No sense in both of us getting in trouble."

Declan turned to leave, then he turned back to me as if he had forgotten something. "El, be careful."

"Declan, he's a priest. What's the worst he can do, condemn my soul to Hell? I've already been exiled to Tory."

Declan chuckled then quickly pecked my cheek before turning toward first hour theology. I trudged the rest of the way to Father Cillian's office alone.

The entrance to the pastor's office was barricaded by an intricately carved iron and oak door. The nameplate was written in raised letters. The script was Gaelic. Had I paid better attention in Professor O'Riley's class, the words may have been readable, but my inaptitude made them impossible to decipher.

I raised my hand to knock just as the door swung inward.

"Ah, Arella, I'm happy ta see that ya haven't changed your mind 'bout my offer." Father Cillian stood in the doorway to his office, waggling his head and smiling like a chubby jack-in-the-box. "And ya remembered your history book. Good, good."

"Just following directions," I replied as he locked his door and ushered me down the hall. "Where are we going?"

"Dún Bhaloir, where Tory's history began of course."

I shrugged my shoulders, not really caring where we went as long as it was away from St. Colm's. "A fieldtrip on the first day--- I like your methods better already."

Father Cillian smiled at me and said, "Ya strike me as one who likes ta experience things first hand, so I'm gonna show ya our history instead of just tellin' ya 'bout it."

We headed out of St. Colm's at a brisk walk. Father Cillian was surprisingly agile for as round as he was. I felt like I had to jog to keep up. "Why are we in such a hurry?"

"Someone is meetin' us and 'twould be rude ta be late."

"Who?" My tone was hard. I was under the impression that these were private lessons, and I was in no mood for extra company.

"Don't ya worry none. It's another student who has been benefitin' from my tutorin'. I'm sure ya'll get on fine together."

Great. Just fabulous. So I was joining another parochial outcast. I stopped trying to keep up with the priest, crossed my arms, and shifted all of my weight to my left hip. "You know, I think that maybe this was a mistake."

Father Cillian stopped midstride and turned to face me. The angry look I expected wasn't there. Instead, the old cleric's face was soft with understanding. "Arella, I know ya want ta leave, but ya can't without the Knowledge."

I waved the ancient volume of Tory history I'd been carrying. "This has no knowledge worth my time. Who cares about the ancient history of a godforsaken island no one wants to visit. How is knowing who settled this rocky crag gonna help me get off it? Don't think you can woo me into liking it here with some made up fairy tales of kings and pirates. I know this place for what it is, a haven for social rejects and fools afraid to live in the real world."

"Well, now," the priest said calmly, "ya're partially correct, but unless ya come with me, ya won't know which part."

I puffed my cheeks and blew out my breath in a frustrated huff. He was right; I really didn't have any other options. "OK, but the first sign that you're trying to convince me that this is where I belong, I'm heading for the nearest dock, and if I can't leave on a ferry, I'll swim the hell out of here."

"Agreed. And your part of the bargain is that ya listen ta the early history of Tory with an open mind."

"Sure," I said, rolling my eyes.

The priest nodded and continued his brisk trot east out of town. We stayed on the main road. After a quarter mile, I was glad I had opted to wear my tennis shoes. I waited for Father Cillian to begin pointing out the many features and monuments of Tory as we passed through An Baile Thiar toward Baile Thoir, but he remained silent. Even when we passed an old World War II torpedo, obviously displayed for history's sake, we passed without comment. Some history teacher.

Finally, we neared the end of the road. I waited for the priest to explain, but he just hurried up the gradual incline leading toward some sort of rocky summit overlooking the ocean. That's when I spotted someone standing on the barren outcropping of limestone facing the mainland. Was this the other pupil Father Cillian had talked about us meeting?

Father Cillian stopped to take a breath then turned to announce, "I believe ya've met Cannon Fidelous before. He has been a private pupil of mine for a few weeks now."

Cannon Fidelous? Just wonderful! So I was set to join the

ranks of Tory Island's outcasts and losers. "Cannon? I thought he hated St. Colms."

"He does, just as ya do, but he seeks the Knowledge."

"Right. So what is this place?"

"Ya've been here before, don't ya know." The old man's eyes gleamed with mischief.

I crossed my arms over my chest, surveying the cleric's smug grin. "No, I don't think so."

"Arella, ya were drawn here yesterday. This is Balor's Fort."

My eyes scanned the rugged terrain leading out into the churning whitecaps of the ocean's gray abyss. The grass under my feet gave way to chalky gravel and jagged stone rising and narrowing into a severe peninsula surrounded on three sides by cliffs ninety meters high. The wind plaited my hair into tangles as it flitted in and out of the damp clefts and fissures of the ancient sediments, and all around me I felt a pulse, an acute vibration surging through the rock, like the flicker of a spirit, the land's very soul quivering with life.

A familiar voice cut in, "This place is the key to our returning home." The absence of the usual Tory brogue caught me off guard. Cannon stood just to my left, a smirk on his face. His dark eyes were wide with excitement. He must be feeling the same vibration.

"If so, why are you still here?" I snapped.

"No, the key is here," Father Cillian pointed to the book I held loosely clutched in my left hand. "We've got ta locate the door ta which it fits."

I shook my head, trying to clear away the mist rising in my logic. "Listen, I didn't come here for a string of fairy tales. You promised to explain why neither one of us is able to leave the island. If you brought me out here to try and convince me that there's some magic door that leads out of this place back to reality, I think I'd rather suffer through Father Dalbach's theology class.

The priest nodded, putting his hands behind his back. "I understand. Ya'll need some convincin' then. I know how ta do that if ya're brave enough."

I looked from Cannon to Father Cillian and back. Both of them wore an aggravating smirk. "Go ahead, convince me," I dared.

Cannon patted the priest on the back. "Allow me, Father."

"Yes, yes, just try not ta shock her too thoroughly."

Cannon chuckled as he beckoned me forward. "Arella, close your eyes."

"Why?"

"Just trust me."

I gave Cannon a sidelong look as I tried to decide whether or not he was pulling something. He raised his eyebrows and held out his hands, waiting for me to comply. I rolled my eyes derisively before closing them. How was Cannon going to prove anything to me when I couldn't see what he was doing?

I heard Father Cillian's warning, "Cannon, ya be careful now."

I felt something grip my waist and pull me off balance. Before I could open my mouth to disperse the string of obscenities weaving in my brain, I found my lips pressed against Cannon's. Anger shot through me like molten lead. You *!#*#! It happened so fast, I didn't think; I just reacted. I raised my knee sharply and listened for a groan.

Nothing.

Fine. He asked for it. I clamped my teeth together and waited for an agonizing scream to erupt from his trapped tongue. Again, nothing. No yelps of pain or shrieked apologies. Instead, the letch just snickered. Jerk!

Pissed off and confused, I opened my eyes, cocked back

my right arm, and let my fist fly right into the center of his sniggering jaw.

Uproarious laughter spewed from his mouth.

"What's wrong with you? Why aren't you groaning in pain and crying for mercy?"

Cannon finally choked out, "It doesn't hurt! Don't you see? You can't hurt me. No one can."

Oh, yeah? I kicked him in the groin again, pretending his crotch was a soccer ball. He responded with another spasm of amusement. I stood still, contemplating his immunity to pain.

"Arella, I can't feel pain. *We* can't feel pain."

What was going on? None of this was making sense. Oh, God! My breath caught in my chest as I remembered falling on the soccer field, hitting my head, but not feeling any pain. I thought of the day I fell on the rocks when I was chasing Declan on the beach near the Cursing Stone's pedestal. I hadn't been hurt, not even a scratch. But what about those damn black patent leather shoes? They're always squishing my feet. Wasn't that pain? Or had I only imagined it?

Cannon held up his arms, calling a truce. He took my left hand and held it palm side up. He traced his fingers over the contours lining it, his thumb resting on a dark purple streak cutting three-fourths its length. "This is your lifeline."

"So?"

"So, haven't you noticed it changing?"

"No." I really hadn't. "What are you getting at?"

"That first day we met, we shook hands. Remember?" I nodded, and Cannon continued. "I knew then that you were like me...alive."

"Of course I'm alive!"

"Arella, just listen. Your hand was really warm like mine, so I turned it over and sure enough you had a lifeline. But that day, it reached all the way across your palm." Cannon rubbed his thumb over the purple streak etched into my skin. "It's shorter now."

"And that means?"

"It means that your time is running out."

"Cannon, stop talking in riddles." I was really at the end of my patience.

Cannon shoved his palm in front of my face. "Look!" he said pointing to a small purple scratch barely an inch long. "I only have a month, maybe less. I can't remember my old life any more. I don't know if I had parents or where I lived. I don't even remember how I got here. All I know is my lifeline is nearly gone. Arella, do you remember your parents? Can you describe your father?"

I grimaced trying to remember. "He's in his fifties. Very brilliant. And he's a theology professor."

"No," Cannon shook his head. "Describe what he looks like."

"He's tall…I think. Gray..grayish hair."

"What color eyes?"

Green, maybe brown. I couldn't remember. "What makes the difference?" I growled.

"Because you can't remember him. Your old life is starting to expire. If you don't find a way to leave Tory soon, your former existence will be nothing more to you than a faded illusion, a dream half-remembered. Arella, your soul is separating from your physical body. You're dying."

"No!" The impact of Cannon's words hit me square in the gut. I looked to Father Cillian.

The old cleric had been standing silently off to the side. His feathery hair floated around his head in the breeze, making his pale features appear ethereal. He cleared his throat, then said, "'Tis true, dear. The shadows, the lights, the fog…all remnants of your physical being. If ya don't repair the fissure between your body and soul soon, they'll be no return."

"How? I don't understand?"

Father Cillian pointed to the book in my hand. "The answer is within those pages. Professor McAnnals and I have been studyin' the text for years. We haven't been able to piece together the clues, but…" His voice trailed off, carried away by a gust of ocean air.

My eyes puckered as I tried to restrain the tears. "But what?"

The old priest shook his head. He held up both of his hands. Both palms were white and smooth. No lines. "I've been on Tory for more than a lifetime. I'll not be leavin' this island, but there's still hope for ya and Cannon."

"Aunt Fi?" I didn't want to know, but I knew I had to ask.

Father Cillian counted back on his fingers. "She's been here since 1975."

"Colin Donland? Brigid Dunn?"

"Twenty-nine years and eighteen years."

"Declan?" I winced as his name slid off of my lips.

"He's been here the longest, since 1884."

I swallowed hard then asked, "Is everyone here dead or dying?" I was remembering the woman and the little girl at the lighthouse.

"No," Father Cillian answered with a frown, "but there is only a thin veil that separates us. We exist side by side without awareness. Ya and Cannon, however, have a foot in each world and are conscious of those existing on both sides."

I covered my face with my hands, digging the heels of my palms into my eyes. No! No! No! This wasn't happening. I was going to wake up and find that it was all just a very bad dream, a horrible hallucination.

Cannon's voice called softly over my shoulder. "Arella, we're going to figure this out. I promise."

I pulled my hands away from my face, balling them into fists ready to strike. I turned on Cannon like a cornered animal. "What makes you think we can figure it out when no one else has?"

"No one else has wanted it so badly. Don't you see? The others never really wanted to leave. They let their lifelines fade because this place was home to them, but you and I don't belong here. We have a life beyond Tory."

I let the tears fall from my eyes. They burned my skin as they descended toward my chin. I watched them, one by one, fall to the ground and soak into the rocky soil. "Where do I begin?"

"Ya must become familiar with Tory's history. Study the book," Father Cillian instructed.

"If the secret is in the book, can't we just find the author and ask him." I was stating the obvious, hoping it would be a simple solution.

"It was written by a man called Mac Gorra who disappeared sometime between 550 and 570 A.D. Legend has it that St. Colm Cille turned him ta stone after he lied ta him. It's in the book."

"How can the legend be in the history book if the man who wrote it was turned to stone?" I then thought of the lessons Professor McAnnals had covered: the Battle of the Bell Tower in 1595, the massacre of sixty refugees seeking asylum on Tory in 1608, and the gifting of Tory to John Stafford in 1655. "How could he have written the book? Most of the things written in here took place after 570."

Father Cillian nodded in understanding. "We now call Mac Gorra's book history because the things written in it have come ta pass. But when it was first penned, it was considered the work of an oracle. Mac Gorra was able ta see Tory's future, don't ya know."

I started flipping through the book's pages. "So are there things in here that haven't happened yet?"

"The last account is the sinking of the HMS Wasp in 1884," the cleric said, avoiding looking me straight in the eye.

1884? The date suddenly clicked in my brain. Hadn't Father Cillian said that Declan arrived on Tory in 1884. And he had been on the island the longest, yet he was no older than Cannon and I. Declan had talked about the HMS Wasp when telling me the legend of the Cursing Stone. Obviously there must be some connection.

Father Cillian patted me reassuringly on the back. "Arella, go home and study the book. We'll meet again tamorrow, same time, at my office door."

"And not a word to anyone about what we've discussed," Cannon added.

"Why not?" If we needed to find the key to escaping Tory before Cannon's and my lifelines faded, shouldn't we try to see if anyone could give us a clue that could help?

"Trust me, Arella, no one else wants this puzzle to be solved. It could end their existence on Tory and possibly anywhere else, for that matter."

I looked at Father Cillian. The sparkle had left his eyes, and a heavy seriousness had settled over his features. "Lass, Professors McAnnals and O'Riley and I are ready ta break this enchantment, but I fear that the others are afraid of the repercussions."

Cannon repeated his warning, "Like I said, Arella, not a word to anyone, especially to Declan."

My stomach was in knots, and my hands were shaking. I nodded in stunned agreement.

Chapter Eight

"So ya thought ya could slip by without me seein' ya, aye?"
I stifled my surprise, trying to act casual. I put my back to the blue cottage door and stuttered, "Hello, Declan, I...I..." Slipping Mac Gorra's book behind me, I faked a smile. "I have a lot of homework. Father Cillian is determined to get me caught up in time for graduation."

"So your lessons went well then?" His stare was incisive, though his gap-toothed smile made his words congenial.

"Yes, they actually did. I think I'm going to like studying with Father Cillian."

Declan nodded, but his eyebrows knitted together, showing his mistrust.

"Well, I'll see you later. I want to get my homework done early, so I better get started." Before Declan could stop me or say another word, I opened the door and slipped inside.

Aunt Fi was humming and painting another watercolor. I didn't stop to announce my return. I went directly to my room, shut the door, and flopped on my bed with a sigh. Rolling over, I flipped through the pages of Mac Gorra's *History of Tory*.

We had covered a few of the chapters in Professor McAnnals' class, but I had had little reason to pay attention then. I turned to the table of contents and began skimming the chapter titles. I was trying to avoid reading the book from cover to cover, but I finally came to the miserable conclusion that I had no other choice. I propped my pillows against my bed's wrought iron backboard and made myself as comfortable as possible for a long night's read.

I yawned my way through the first thirty pages of Mac

Gorra's account, fighting to keep my eyes open and my mind focused. In the first chapter, he started with the legend of Tory's early Nemedian settlers and progressed to the murder of Balor of the Evil Eye by his own grandson. The second chapter talked about St. Colm Cille and the monastery he founded on Tory in the sixth century, as well as the many miracles and legends surrounding him. In all truth, the book read more like a fairy tale than a history book. After a couple hours of tedium, I closed the book and shut my eyes.

Crek-crek.

It was back. I sat up on my bed more than a little irritated. Was this feral chicken going to be pestering me from now on? I grabbed my shoe and stalked to the window, ready to scare off the nuisance. "Get out of here, shoo!" I yelled, throwing open the window.

Crek-crek. Crek-crek. Crek-crek.

Great! In the grass below my window was not one, but three corncrakes. Didn't Declan say these birds were shy and rarely seen?

Crek-crek. Crek-crek-crek. Crek.

I slammed the window shut and turned my back on their agitated squawks. That's when I noticed the picture. Aunt Fi must have finished another watercolor for me. Next to my family picture and the painting of Tory lighthouse hung a watercolor of a rocky cliff jutting out into the foaming sea. It was obviously Balor's fort. The painting was magnificent; the lines were bold, and the colors were full of depth. The rendering made the craggy peninsula rise out of the picture as though the canvas was a window overlooking the actual landform. I half-expected the bird flying across its sky to flap its way into my room.

El. El, ya must go.

Knock, knock. "El?"

"What?"

Declan's voice called through the door. "Can I come in?"

I grabbed my history book as I replied. "Declan, I really have a lot of studying to do."

"Don't ya know the sayin', 'All work and no play…'?"

Sigh. I went to the door and opened it a crack. There stood Declan, green eyes dancing behind a mischievous, crooked smile.

He moved toward me, easing his way through the opening. "There's a céili tonight at the club. Ya promised ya'd come with me."

"Oh, Declan, I can't."

His eyes darkened as his smile melted into a pout. I tipped my head to the side, letting my bangs hide the color rising in my cheeks.

Declan leaned against the door jam. "Father Cillian must be quite a teacher ta have ya so committed ta your studies." His jaw tightened, and his eyes scanned back and forth reading my poorly shielded guilt.

Dejection crowded his features. Crimony! What if Cannon and Father Cillian were wrong about Declan? I threw my history book on my bed and blurted out, "Give me five minutes to change."

Declan's crooked smile returned. "I promise it'll be worth it." He rolled off of the door jam and disappeared down the hall.

I took a deep breath and flung open my closet door. What do you wear to a céi…céil… a frickin' Irish dance? I flung several pairs of jeans and at least ten different blouses onto my bed before I settled on a denim miniskirt and matching jacket. I accented the dark blue with a white t-shirt and several necklaces --dangling Celtic crosses and various other secular silver charms on black leather cords. I shimmied a pair of black leggings under my skirt and slipped on a pair of red tennis shoes, the kind with really thick soles and white rubber over the toes. I ran a quick comb through my hair before pulling it back loosely in a barrette. Ok, not perfect, but presentable.

I guess Declan approved because, when I joined him in the living room, he stuttered, "Ya look...really...great. I...us...we better be goin' now. I promise ta have 'er back before ten, Miss Cline." He gripped my arm and guided me through the front door and out onto the street before Aunt Fi could do more than chuckle and wave.

As we walked to town, Declan filled me in on all I had missed at St. Colm that day. First, he explained how Colin Donland had burped obscenely loud in Father Dalbach's class just as the priest was explaining that the fourth commandment, honor your father and mother, should be applied to all those in authority. It earned him an after school detention writing out Proverb 15:33, *The fear of the Lord is the instruction of wisdom, and before honor is humility*, one hundred and fifty times.

Then he explained that Brigid Dunn was caught cheating on her Gaelic exam. Professor O'Riley told her she would have to translate the entire first chapter of the 12th Century Book of Invasions of Ireland if she did not want to repeat the class next year. Despite myself, I felt sorry for the girl.

Finally, Declan told me that Professor McAnnals had a substitute teaching her class. It wouldn't have been a big deal, except that the professor hadn't missed a day since coming to St. Colm, and no one remembers how long ago she started there. The substitute was a weasly little man with a high-pitched voice. His name was Iollan McGradey.

"Well, it sounds like the place has really gone to the dogs without me."

Declan stopped walking. "El, nothin' is right without ya." He looked down at his feet, embarrassed. "I kept lookin' for ya in the halls, and walkin' home alone felt like the longest trek I've ever taken. Why don't ya reconsider?"

"Declan," I forced out a breath, hoping to release the frustration building inside, "I can't."

"But why? You can drop theology class but still attend St. Colm's for your other subjects." His eyes were watery as he pleaded with me.

I blinked back tears and slowly shook my head. "Declan, don't ask me to do that. Studying with Father Cillian is the right thing for me. Please understand."

Declan took my right hand into both of his. He raised it to his lips and kissed the tips of my fingers. A cold chill rippled over me, raising my skin into gooseflesh. My heart thudded against my ribcage. The night's cool air was suddenly stifling.

"El, don't ya miss me?"

Oh, God! I could feel myself melting right there into the dirt road. I started to move my lips, but no sound came out. Declan kissed my fingers again before sliding his lips to my wrist.

"Declan," I managed to sigh, "Are you trying to seduce me back to the Academy?" I was starting to waver. I could feel my knees as well as my resolve give way.

"Seduce sounds evil," Declan continued. "Charm is more like it." He looked up from my wrist, his lips still gliding over my racing pulse.

Crimony! He was good. And I was weakening. I had to regain composure, and fast, or I was done.

Declan must have known he had me, because just then he took both of my hands and held them palm side up. He ran his thumbs over the lines criss-crossing my skin, trying to hide the fact that he was studying the length of my lifeline. I knew exactly what he was doing, and it totally ruined the mood. I pulled my hands away.

"El?"

Cripe, he was persistent! "Declan, please."

He brushed back my bangs with his hand then rested his chilly palm against my cheek. When his green eyes delved into mine, it was like two hypnotic kaleidoscopes of light overwhelming my sense of awareness. He whispered, "El, I can't bear ta be without ya."

He could have kissed me right there, and it would have been all over. I would have promised to reenroll at St. Colms, attend Father Dalbach's class, and even be best friends with Brigid Dunn. Yet, Declan knew how to keep me hanging on, just like a fish being played on a line. "We're missin' the céili, and I promised ya the time of your life. Let's go." He gave me a wink and pulled me down the road at a trot.

Boy, he was good! For the rest of the night my eyes followed him like I was a love starved puppy. Club na Maighdine Mara was packed with many familiar faces, but I couldn't draw my attention away from Declan for two seconds. As he led me from group to group introducing me and chatting casually, I couldn't stop looking at the curve of his mouth and the line of his jaw. Even when Colin Donland asked me to dance a simple Irish reel with him, I couldn't concentrate on the steps. I kept stealing glances at Declan and tripping over my own feet. Finally, the poor guy gave up, saying, "Arella, ya're gonna kill us both if ya don't stop gawkin' at Declan."

I gave Colin a remorseful smile. "Sorry, I don't know what's come over me."

"I do. He's charmed ya. There's no fightin' it. Ya might as well give in."

I nodded my gratitude for his understanding and zigzagged across the crowded dance floor back toward Declan. I was only a couple of yards away from where he was standing against the wall talking with Keenan and Bryce, two of the soccer players from our pickup game, when Brigid Dunn pushed her way past an elderly couple to cut me off. I heard her giggle as she wrapped her arms around one of his and led him to the dance floor, and I could swear a snide smirk flickered over the corner of her mouth when her eye caught my stare.

What a wench! My eyes dug virtual wounds into her giddy head as she pranced around the room in Declan's arms. Ugh! I wanted to scream! As my insides began to seethe with contempt, I realized I had to leave immediately or I would surely cause an ugly scene. I pressed blindly through the throng of dancers jigging to the reedy sounds of the melodeon players. I desperately needed to reach the exit before my fury detonated.

"Aye, Arella. Want ta dance?" It was Sean, the goalie from the pickup soccer game.

"I, uh… I need to get some air, but thanks." I was out the door just in time. Angry tears exploded from my eyes the moment the cool night air touched my face. I smeared the moisture with the back of my hand as I choked back a loud sob.

I knew I was being stupid about Brigid, but I couldn't help it. There was something about that girl that grated on me like stone on steel, and to see her carrying on like that with Declan was just too much to take. Colin was right; Declan had some kind of hold on me, and every time I tried to shake free, his invisible fingers closed tighter. I had to get a grip.

Take a walk, El. Ròm Sarut Na.

"What? Dad? Is that you? What are you trying to tell me?" I stared into the darkness, expecting my father's shadow to emerge from the growing darkness.

"El? There ya are. Let's take a walk." Declan's voice startled me, and I jumped a foot in the air. "Why are ya cryin'?" he asked when I turned to face him.

I roughly rubbed the sleeve of my jacket over my wet cheeks. "I'm not crying. I'm just a little flushed. It was getting stuffy in there." I pointed to the club door. The sounds of fiddles and drums overflowed its hinges.

"Ya weren't enjoyin' the céili?" The corners of his mouth turned down in disappointment.

"Well, maybe it's just not my thing."

"Well, I promised ya a good time. I don't want ta disappoint ya." He wrapped his hand around mine and started leading me down the dirt road toward the shore.

"That's all right, Declan." I tried to pull my hand free. "I should just be going home anyway. I still have studying to do. You can go back to the céili. I can walk myself home."

Declan held my hand firmly. "Not before I show ya somethin'."

I was in no mood for another fieldtrip. "Can't it wait 'til morning?" I had desperately wanted Declan's attention just minutes before, but now I only wanted to be alone.

"No. Come on now."

I sighed loudly but let Declan lead me to the pier. We walked across the weather-worn planks together. He gripped my hand firmly as he swung it playfully back and forth. I didn't resist, though I had a slight niggling in the back of my head telling me I should. When we got to the end, Declan grabbed my other hand and turned me toward him.

The moon above was nearly full, and its light glinted off of the water sending illuminated ripples across the black shimmering surface. A crisp breeze blew into shore, carrying with it the scent of salt and seaweed. It played with the loose ends of my hair. The pale clouds above sailed across the sky in a silent race to midnight.

Declan's eyes were brilliant emeralds in the darkness. I blinked trying to avert the spell.

He broke his own enchantment. "Ya know that Brigid is just a friend. Her askin' me ta dance was all in good fun. I would've rather been asked by ya, El."

I looked away, focusing on a single star burning in the sky. It was a tiny pinprick of light, but its intensity made up for its size. "You can dance with whomever you like. It's not my business." I stuck out my chin in stubborn finality.

"El," Declan took my chin in his hand, raising my eyes to meet his. "I didn't want ta dance with Brigid. Why didn't ya ask me?"

I shook my head. "Hold on there. Isn't that the guy's job? You know, to be all chivalrous and what not. Why didn't you ask me?"

"All right, will ya honor me with this dance, Arella Cline?" He put out his arms waiting for me to accept.

After a moment of silence, I burst out laughing. I couldn't help it; I felt awkward and embarrassed. "Forget it. I'm going home. Listen, I had fun tonight anyway."

I started walking back across the pier, but Declan grabbed my hand and pulled me back toward him. "What…" I couldn't finish the sentence. His mouth was against mine, his lips enticing me to respond back. His kiss was gentle, and when he pulled away, I was left wishing he hadn't.

"I have somethin' I want ta give ta ya. It belonged ta my grandmother." Declan reached into his pocket and retrieved a silver hair comb. Moonlight glinted off of its surface, showing it was delicately inlaid with tiny crystals.

"Oh, Declan, it's gorgeous! But I can't take it."

Declan leaned in and kissed me again. His lips were cool, but they left me burning when he broke away. "Yes, ya can." He held up the comb, offering it to me.

My fingers reached for it. *Crek-crek!* I jerked my hand back in surprise. *Crek-crek! Crek-crek!* A flurry of feathers flew between us. One, two, three, at least four corncrakes flapped chaotically around us. *Crek-crek! Crek-crek-crek!* Their urgent squawking sent a frightening chill through me. I spun around, waving my arms over my head trying to knock them away. *Thup, thup, thup.* The sound of their beating wings drummed in my ears. I threw myself into a crouch low to the ground, protecting my head with my arms.

Bits of down drifted through the air as silence settled around us. I uncovered my head to chance a look around. Declan was brushing feathers out of his hair, a sardonic grimace on his face. When he had removed most of the debris clinging to him, he helped me to my feet.

"I don't…" I stopped in midsentence, my eye caught by an unexpected glimmer. The silver hair comb must have fallen to the ground in the midst of the corncrake commotion. It lay abandoned on the pier in a gap between two warped planks. I bent down to pick it up.

"Stop! Don't touch it!"

Declan and I turned in unison in the direction the warning had come. Cannon Fidelous was racing toward us, waving his arms in alarm.

Declan ordered, "El, take the comb." His voice was impatient, full of desperation, and his look that went with it was frightening.

I reached for the comb with shaking fingers. I felt compelled to obey.

"No!" Cannon yelled again. Then he pushed me, and I fell over onto my hip.

"Cannon, what the…"

However, it was too late to say anything. Cannon stomped on the comb, forcing it through the planks. I scrambled to catch it, but all I could do was watch as it hit the inky water below, sinking out of sight.

"Ya dog!" Declan lunged at Cannon, knocking him on his back. The two of them rolled back and forth, taking turns throwing punches.

"Both of you stop it! Stop!" I tried to pull them apart, but it was like trying to stop a pit bull fight. Both of them were crazed beyond reason. I was afraid they would forget who they were fighting and turn on me, so I backed away and watched hopelessly as they beat one another senseless.

"All right now. That's enough." Father Cillian scuttled out of the shadows. "I'll not be toleratin' ya boys actin' like a couple of hoodlums now. Break it up."

Surprisingly, Declan and Cannon complied without complaint. However, they eyed one another with such obvious hatred, I was certain they would launch into another battle at any second. For a moment, I was shocked that neither boy was hurt until I remembered that that was impossible.

Father Cillian's eyes narrowed. "Now, what is this all about?"

Cannon blurted out, "Declan tried to trick Arella into taking a silver hair comb."

"Is that so, Declan McQuilan?" the priest asked.

"Wait," I interrupted, "Declan was trying to give me a gift. He wasn't trying to trick me at all. Why are you both looking at him like he was doing something wrong?"

"Because he was," Cannon seethed. "Arella, don't you know what picking up a silver hair comb does?"

I crossed my arms over my chest. "No," I said in my most disgusted voice.

"It calls the banshees." Cannon's face twisted in horror. "Once they get a hold of you, there's no hope of return. They're the Irish angels of death, so to speak."

"Right! Now ya expect her to believe in death fairies. Piss off, Cannon." Declan grabbed my hand, pulling me toward him.

"Arella, I'm not lying," Cannon spoke in a pleading voice.

Declan tried to lead me away, but I turned to look at

Cannon. His eyes were wide with honesty. I wanted to believe him, but I didn't want to believe Declan was trying to trick me either. I turned to Father Cillian.

The old cleric nodded. "'Tis long been a myth in Ireland."

"A myth," Declan spat out, "not fact. Ya're scarin' Arella with your ridiculous legends. El, what else have they told ya?"

"Um…well…" I looked from Father Cillian to Cannon and back again, wanting a sign as to what I should say. Father Cillian didn't look at me. He just closed his eyes and put his hands together as if he were praying. Cannon drew his lips together in a thin line but said nothing.

Declan took my hands in his and held my gaze. His eyes reflected the moon's light. I felt my pulse quiver as he began to speak. "El, they're talkin' nonsense. Come on now, banshees? And why would I try ta hurt ya? I care 'bout ya. I was only tryin' ta give ya a gift ta show ya how I feel. I…I think I'm in love with ya, El."

Love? The word rolled off of Declan's tongue like honey dripping from a spoon, sticky sweet and messy. Inside my chest, my heart thumped so hard I thought I was going to pass out. But inside my gut, something said run.

"Love? You're the real dog," Cannon said, disgust spilling out with every word. "You'd toy with her like that? There's not a lick of humanity left in you, is there? You've forgotten what it's like to feel anything, let alone love. Man, you suck!"

"I'm not toyin' with her. I love her," Declan insisted.

My muscles felt weak, and my breathing started to come in quick gasps. I looked at Declan, trying to focus my thoughts, but his crooked smile got in the way. Was he telling the truth, or was Cannon? I shook my head, no longer able to separate reality from fantasy. "I've gotta go."

"What?" the boys blurted out almost in unison.

"I've got studying to do. Father Cillian, same time

tomorrow?"

The priest nodded, "Aye, I'll be waitin'."

I took one more longing look at Declan's disappointed face, gave him a weak smile, nodded to Cannon, and then hurried back over the pier toward shore.

When I got back to the cottage, Aunt Fi was still awake. She was in the parlor working on another painting.

She turned as I entered the room. "Ah, Arella dear, did ya enjoy yerself at the céili?

"Yeah," I lied, not about to elaborate on banshees and fist fights.

"I finished another paintin' for ya," she said with a soft smile. "It's in your room."

"Thanks," I said, a little bewildered. "I've got studying to do. See you in the morning, Aunt Fi." I kissed her on the cheek and went directly to my room.

Sure enough, hanging on my wall with my family portrait, the painting of Tory Lighthouse, and the picture of Balor's Fort was another watercolor. In its forefront was the ocean, and in the background was a nondescript grassy field interspersed with rock. In the center, the subject of the picture was a large slab of gray stone. What a strange and boring object to paint. The rock was shaped into a rectangle. It looked to be a representation of some sort of table or altar hewn out of granite. Three holes or wells were carved into the top. A shimmer of color made it look like the wells held water. Lovely. Why would Aunt Fi paint me a picture of a rock?

I rolled my eyes, dismissing my aunt's present as a product of the onset of senility. Huh, maybe I was the one going crazy.

I flopped on the bed and reached for Mac Gorra's *History of Tory*. The book was lying open at the foot of my bed. It was opened to the two pages that looked like a maze. I started to flip to the chapter where I had left off reading before going to the céili, but something caught my eye--the words *Ròm Sarut Na* written in fancy script at the top.

Ròm Saurt Na? Where had I heard that before? *Ròm Sarut Na. Ròm Sarut Na.* Suddenly I remembered. My father's voice had said those same words.

I studied the intricate swirls adorning the two pages, trying to figure out what they meant. Interspersed among the swirls were tiny pictures that reminded me of the hieroglyphics in low -budget mummy movies. The whole thing looked like an elaborate maze.

Maze? Maybe. Why not? I stretched, grabbing a pencil off my dresser. Where was the starting point? For that matter, where was the ending point? There was a little glyph resembling a fat *T.* I started there. I scratched my pencil around the swirls and through the elaborate pattern of lines. After tracing and retracing, erasing, and backtracking, my graphite line finally met up with where I had started. Great! I had made a complete lopsided circle through the mishmash of twisting and turning lines and glyphs right back to the fat little *T.* I know; it was a metaphor for my life, one big mixed-up, never-ending circle of confusion. No beginning and no end in sight.

I slammed the book shut and tossed it under my bed. Fighting back a yawn, I quickly changed into a t-shirt and pajama pants and climbed under the homemade quilt. I flicked off the light and closed my eyes, hoping sleep would rescue me from the night's insanity.

Chapter Nine

Crek-crek. Crek-crek.

Oh, shut up! I threw my pillow at the window and rolled over.

Crek-crek. Crek.

Cripes! I kicked off my covers and stormed out of bed. I jerked the shade with a little too much muscle, sending it up with a smack. One, two, three, four, five, six...seven. Seven corncrakes sat huddled beneath my window, squawking and fretting back and forth. Terrific! They were multiplying! I looked up at the swirling sky. It was shrouded by gray storm clouds. Just another day in paradise.

I turned away from the flock of complaining fowl and quickly got dressed in jeans and a wool sweater. I pulled on a pair of boots, sure that the clouds' promise of rain would be fulfilled while I was out on lecture with Father Cillian.

Before leaving my room, I lay flat on the floor, reached under the bed, and groped for my history book. I retrieved it, along with a wad of dust-bunnies. The dog-eared corners of Mac Gorra's book looked as though they probably contributed to the puff of dust rising from the disturbance. Ruefully, I wondered what would fade away first, my lifeline or the pages of Mac Gorra's history.

"Arella, ya're off early taday." Aunt Fi was in her usual spot, in front of her easel and paints in the parlor.

"Yeah, couldn't sleep."

"I'm paintin' ya another picture, lass."

Another one? "Gee, thanks Aunt Fi, but you don't have to. My room looks real...homey now. The walls aren't bare anymore."

"Oh, ya'll like this one," she said as her strokes became wider.

"What is it?" I stepped toward the easel, my curiosity peaked.

Aunt Fi shooed me away. "Ya'll just have ta wait. It'll be finished when ya return. Ya can see it then."

I shrugged off her secrecy and headed for the door. Grabbing my raincoat from its hook on the mudroom wall, I went outside. The air was damp and cold. I zipped up my coat, drew up the hood, and pulled my hands into the sleeves as far as they would go. I shoved my free hand into a deep pocket. My other hand held Tory's voluminous history, so I was quickly resolved to the fact that those knuckles would be red and chapped.

I got to Father Cillian's door ten minutes before I was expected. I hesitated outside his door, wondering whether I should knock or wait. I didn't want to chance running into Declan just then, so I knocked.

"Come in," Father Cillian called through the door.

I turned the heavy brass knob until it clicked. The door groaned inward.

The old cleric greeted me with an eager smile. "Ah, Arella, ya're early. Impatient ta begin your lessons?"

I shrugged my shoulders. "A flock of noisy corncrakes woke me up. I couldn't get back to sleep."

Father Cillian nodded. "Well, did ya have a chance ta study Mac Gorra's history?" The priest leaned back in his chair, the tips of his fingers touching together into a tent under his chin.

"I tried, but I didn't get far. I'm just not into dates and dead people."

The priest eyed me with intense interest before replying, "Somewhere in those pages is the answer ya're lookin' for. Are ya willin' ta put forth the effort?"

I crossed my arms over my chest and let my bangs shroud my face, my usual reaction to uncomfortable situations.

"Well, are ya, Arella Cline?"

I shook the hair out of my face before answering, "I don't know what I'm willing to do. I don't know if I should do anything. None of this maskes sense--the book, this island, me on this island."

"Well, ya best figure it out before ya're put ta the test."

I studied the old man's face. His eyes were soft with understanding, but his mouth was pressed together in a serious line of thought. I let my gaze roam the room, trying to avoid his scrutiny. That's when I saw it.

On a bookshelf along the wall, being used as a bookend for a number of dusty volumes, I saw a sculpture with a remarkable resemblance to the strange *T* glyph in my book. I immediately flipped through the age-worn pages of Tory's history until I came to the pair labeled *Ròm Sarut Na*. My eyes went from the book to the sculpture and back again. They were the same.

I ignored Father Cillian's ramblings as I went to the shelf to examine the piece more closely. It was actually a carving. The stone was dark with age and worn smooth to the touch. I took it from the shelf and held it up to the priest. "What is this?"

Father Cillian stopped in mid-lecture. "What?"

I waved the stone *T* in front of him. "What is this carving of?"

"An Chros Tau, the T Cross."

"I've seen it before."

"Aye, it's in West Town. It's one of only two such crosses in Ireland. The other is in Kilnaboy."

"It's here in the book, also." I placed my copy of *The History* on the priest's desk and pointed to the *T* glyph.

"Well, well, I do believe ya've found somethin' I've

overlooked at least a hundred times. I never associated that little smudge with An Chros Tau."

"Then these other symbols must represent other Tory landmarks." I pointed to the other glyphs scattered over the two pages labeled *Ròm Sarut Na*. "Look, it's like a maze of some kind, but there is no beginning or end. I started at the *T*, but it just makes a loop. And what does the title mean? It must be Gaelic, right?"

Father Cillian's brow wrinkled into a dozen folds as he studied the pages. "'Tis no Gaelic I know. And look here." He pointed to a minute inscription beneath an icon resembling a chalice. "And here." He pointed to another symbol in the shape of a tower. "What are these letters? I can't read them. The print is too small."

I leaned close to the page and read off the letters under the chalice, "E, D, I, R, H, B I, A, L, U. Edirhb Ialu? What's that?"

Father Cillian shook his head. "Read off the letters under the T Cross."

"U, A, T S, O, R, H, C N, A. Uat Sorhc Na." I looked up at the old priest and waited for him to translate.

Father Cillian stood, straightening his back as he folded his thick fingers together over his wide torso. He paced around his desk, talking to himself, repeating the letters over and over. He scratched the white fluff on his head before sitting back in his chair with a bump, still muttering the random syllables to himself.

"Maybe it's written in some lost language. You know, elfish or leprechaun tongue." I gave the priest a mischievous smile, but he had his eyes closed in concentration.

Figuring he didn't want to be disturbed, I helped myself to a glass of water from a crystal pitcher on the mahogany sideboard. After taking a half-hearted sip, I set the glass down on the desk and continued staring at the indecipherable pages in front of me.

Several more moments passed before Father Cillian's lips stopped moving, and his eyes opened. He dabbed his forehead with a handkerchief from his coat pocket and stared at me regretfully across the desk. His eyes fell away from mine, settling on the glass of water.

I felt sorry for the old man. He was trapped here. Even if we found a way to leave the island, he was probably doomed to stay or fade into nonexistence. His lifeline was gone and so was his chance of ever departing Tory Island.

"An Chros Tau." He said the words slowly as though each syllable was an arduous chore. "An Chros Tau!" He jumped up from his chair, nearly shouting. "Arella, the words are written backward! Look, the water in the glass magnified and mirrored the letters."

I leaned over the book. Sure enough An Chros Tau had been written backward under the *T* glyph.

Father Cillian's face was flushed with excitement. "Edìrhb Ìalu, the inscription under the challis is Ulaí Bhríde or the Oratory of St. Brigid. Look! The title of these pages is *An Turas Mór*, the mainlanders' pilgrimage. This is a map of the pilgrimage route with all of the holy sites marked by the various glyphs."

"That's great, but how does that help us?"

"Arella, when the Cursin' Stone was stolen in 1884, Tory was put under a spell of enchantment. Someone had made the last An Turas Mór with the specific intent of castin' a curse. No one could leave the island ever again."

"That's not true. My father left the island after he graduated from St. Colm Cille."

"He knew how ta go 'round the curse."

"Terrific." I flopped back down in the chair. "My father is gone, so we're on our own with figuring out this curse thing."

"Well, at least we know 'tis possible."

I looked at my lifeline. It looked like it had receded further. I took a pen from the priest's desk and marked where it ended on either end of my palm. I would have to keep closer watch from now on.

"OK, so why is everything written backward?" I questioned the priest as we made our way to Balor's Fort to meet Cannon.

"Don't know. That's what we have ta find out," Father Cillian answered in between labored breaths.

We had just stepped off Tory's main road and were starting our ascent up the rough trail to Balor's Fort. The climb was steep and jagged, a challenge for me let alone an elderly priest. "And how are we going to do that out here?" I looked across the windswept peninsula, nothing but moss and rock all around. It was beginning to drizzle, and I felt chilled.

The priest stopped trudging the narrow, stony path to look at me. "Have ya heard of the Leac na Leannán, the Wishin' Stone?"

"Yes," I answered, my mind going back to the day Professor Eoin O'Riley had advised me to go see it. I remembered Declan had gotten upset when I asked him to show it to me. "You're not saying that you believe it really is a wishing stone with magical powers, are you?" I let out an amused chuckle.

"Well now, that depends on what ya consider magical." Father Cillian punctuated his statement with a wink before turning to continue the trek.

"Must you always talk in riddles? What are you getting at?" My amusement was slowly turning into irritation.

Father Cillian ignored my questions. He was panting now, straining to continue his climb upward. When the track finally leveled off, I was surprised to see Cannon waiting for us on a stone outcropping. His knees were bent to his chin, his arms wrapped around them. His jaw and cheekbones were locked in a pensive profile. The wind blew through his hair, creating a halo of amber disarray. I closed my eyes. A faint blue and turquoise aura sputtered in front of my lids. Around the edges was a faint glow of white. When I opened my eyes again, Cannon was staring at me, his dark eyes ringed with shadows.

"Cannon, good news," Father Cillian gasped. He bent over, his hands on his knees as he tried to catch his breath. "Arella has partially deciphered a map of the An Turas Mór that Mac Gorra included in his history." The old priest wiped his brow with his handkerchief before standing upright. "I think it has clues ta eradicatin' the curse."

Cannon's sallow expression did not change. "It shrunk again."

"Here, look." The elderly cleric took the book from my hands and leafed to the map. He held out the volume for Cannon's inspection.

"Didn't you hear me? My lifeline shrunk. It's barely visible."

"So quick?" I grabbed Cannon's hand to examine it. Sure enough, his lifeline was no more than a tiny dash on his palm.

"That fight with Declan must have done something. I donno, but we better do something fast, or I'll be stuck here."

"I think we're close, lad. Look." Father Cillian pointed out the icons and explained what we had concluded in his office. "Now we have ta figure out why everythin' is written backwards. I think that is the answer ta breakin' the curse and gettin' ya two home."

Cannon shook his head. "So why are we here at Balor's Fort?"

"We need ta climb ta the Wishin' Stone." Father Cillian pointed to a large flat rock balanced precariously atop a jutting cliff at the end of the peninsula.

"To make a wish?" I asked.

Cannon scowled, "You think a lousy stone is the answer to this? You want us to climb to the top of some cliff and wish ourselves home? Come on."

"No, I want ya ta climb up there ta get the best view of Tory. 'Tis the island's highest point. We need ta see what this map is showin' us."

I let my eyes scan the treacherous path leading across the isthmus. It was the one and only route to the Wishing Stone, and it stretched across a narrow neck of land rising ninety meters out of the sea. Angry waves assaulted the base of the peninsula, while a stiff north wind blustered over the top. I glanced down at my shrinking lifeline and back to the mystical stone looming in the distance. If I fell from the highest point on Tory, would I truly be immune to a ninety meter drop into the ocean?

Cannon swore under his breath. "Fine, but I've been all over this island. I can't see how climbing up there is going to show me anything I haven't seen before."

"Oh, ya'd be surprised how a different perspective can open one's eyes, lad." Father Cillian winked at me then proceeded to lead the way up the stony trail.

"I think the old man's finally lost the last of his marbles," Cannon whispered as the old cleric labored up the slope in front of us. "Maybe after so long on this island, you just completely lose touch with reality and begin to live in Never-Never Land."

"Look who's talking. You're the one who believes in banshees." I couldn't help myself. Cannon set himself up for that one.

He glared at me through the corner of his eye but refrained from responding. I'm not sure if he was considering his sanity or thinking of a way to get back at me. Either way, I was sorry I had said it. I didn't know what to believe either, and I could feel my own judgment wavering on the brink of insanity.

The path leading up to the Wishing Stone was steep. We were forced to use our hands to help us along. At first we merely grabbed hold of a stone here or there to help balance ourselves, but soon we were climbing on all fours to make our slow advance. The wind increased its velocity, but the drizzle remained constant, a nuisance but not a hindrance.

"This better be worth the climb," Cannon called from behind me.

Father Cillian called back over his shoulder, "The view from Leac na Leannán will be."

"You've been up here before?" I asked.

"It's..." He paused to take a breath. "It's been some time, but, aye, when I was young, I climbed ta the top."

The old priest had me curious now. "What did you wish for?"

He turned around and smiled. His eyes were watery and full of regret. "I wished ta live forever."

The irony of the priest's words hit hard, knocking me off balance. I realized in that moment that I had often thrown out similar careless wishes, unaware of the bearing they could have on my life if they were to come true. I tripped over my next step almost falling backward. Cannon caught my elbow and steadied me. I looked down the way we had climbed; it was a long trek back. I took a deep breath and stabilized myself before pressing on.

After more than thirty minutes of struggling against gravity and the elements, we were finally at the base of the alleged magical stone. It was a huge chunk of gray rock balanced at the end of the isthmus, perched precariously above the icy waves beating the rocks below. Its top was flat, peppered with stones of various shapes, sizes, and colors--no doubt the remnants of brave wish seekers. Encrusted with lichen and moss, it appeared impervious to our presence and immune to its surroundings. It was ancient and unyielding in its stance against the passing of time.

"How are we supposed to climb up there?" Cannon asked. His mouth twisted to one side of his face as he surveyed the nearly ninety.degree angle of the boulder's sides.

"We aren't. Arella will, with us as her steppin' stones."

Cannon eyed me dubiously. "How much do you weigh?"

I stuck out my tongue then punched his arm for asking.

"Cannon, stand with your back ta the stone, like so," Father Cillian said as he leaned against the massive chunk of limestone supporting the Wishing Stone. "Now, Arella, climb up on our shoulders. We'll boost ya up ta the top."

"That's great, but how am I supposed to get down once I'm done up there?" My eyes kept looking over the steep sides of the isthmus. I involuntarily kicked a loose stone with the toe of my boot. It sent a mini avalanche of small rocks careening over the edge, and I couldn't help imagining myself among the rubble.

"You could just wish yourself down." Cannon smirked at his own joke.

"Yeah, if I'm gonna chance making a wish, I wouldn't waste it on asking to be placed back down on a desolate land bridge. Just brace yourselves so I don't fall."

Both Father Cillian and Cannon pushed their backs against the limestone and locked their legs in place. They cupped their hands in front of themselves and waited for me to step up.

I gripped their shoulders as I hoisted myself upward, using their hands as steps. When both of my feet were clear of the ground, I braced my legs and felt myself being pushed skyward. My fingers clawed the rough stone, searching for a place to hold on. I managed to force the tips of my fingers into a tiny crevice where lichen had cleaved the rock, giving myself a bit of false security. My head was even with the top of the boulder, but I couldn't see over it.

I called down, "Push up just a few more inches."

My request was answered by a series of grunts and an abrupt upward thrust. The last of the limestone perch passed before my eyes. I could then see over the top of Leac na Leannán. I struggled to raise my elbows to its flat surface. Using my forearms as levers, I lifted the rest of my body onto the stone's crown. I knelt on a jumble of loose rocks, my knees scraping over the shards of previous wishes. I stumbled to my feet, clapping the dirt from my hands.

"What do ya see, Arella?" Father Cillian called.

I turned around in a circle, peering through the mist that was settling around me like a soggy blanket. "Not much. I mean, I can see some of Tory's landmarks like the lighthouse and the pier, but the drizzle is making it hard to pick out any sort of details. What should I be looking for anyway?"

"I'm not sure. Perhaps ya should just describe all that ya can see. We might be able ta pick out somethin' that sounds noteworthy."

"Yeah, sure." Like there was anything noteworthy about this desolate chunk of rock other than it was impossible to leave it. "I can see East Town and West Town and the main road running through them. There's the Academy. I can see St. Colm's bell tower, and there's the Tau Cross. That's pretty much it."

"Can ya see anythin' that looks out of place?"

"How should I know? You should be the one up here. I don't know what to look for."

The drizzle turned into a steady rain. I kept squinting into the gray air hoping something noteworthy would soon catch my attention so we could leave. I mumbled aloud, "Jeez, I wish

Mac Gorra had left a clue."

"Nice, Arella, you just blew a perfectly good wish on asking for a stupid clue. You should have just wished us home." Cannon mocked.

"Well, maybe if I believed this was really a magic stone, I would have. Why don't you haul your butt up here and make your own wish if you can do it better?"

I closed my eyes against the rain, muttering a number of choice words under my breath. In that moment a flash of red flamed behind my eyelids. I reopened my eyes expecting to see something burning right in front of my face; instead, there were only clouds and the rain. I shut my eyes once more, and the red blaze reappeared. "Father Cillian?" I pointed to a section of land jutting off the north side of Tory. "What's over there?"

"Oh, that be Mac Gorra, don't ya know."

"Mac Gorra? The author of *The History*?"

"Well, what's left of 'em. Ya see, tradition has it that Mac Gorra met Colm Cille one Sunday after he'd been fishin'. The good saint asked the man if he had any fish ta spare. Mac Gorra lied and said he hadn't any. St. Colm turned the man ta stone for this sin, and that's where he remains, forever climbin' Mearnaid with his bag of fish on his back."

"Something's there. I mean, I think what we're looking for is hidden somewhere near where Mac Gorra was turned to stone."

Cannon interjected, "Now hold on. What makes you think that?"

I leaned over the edge of the Wishing Stone and smiled at Cannon through dripping locks. "I think Mac Gorra just granted my wish."

Chapter Ten

"So now we have to trek through the rain all the way to Mearnaid?" Cannon whined as we sloshed back across the isthmus.

"Do ya have a better idea now?" Father Cillian glared at Cannon, instantly silencing his next whine.

"Listen, I don't know why, but I've been seeing lights, colors really, when I close my eyes. I don't know what they mean exactly, but I think the red light I saw when looking toward Mearnaid is a sign." The heel of my boot landed on a soggy patch of moss. I skidded a little but kept my balance.

"Ya're seein' auras, Arella." Father Cillian answered as if it were an everyday occurrence.

"So I'm not going crazy or haven't been infected with some rare disease?"

"No, not at all. In fact, it is a rare gift that ya have."

"A gift I really don't know how to use."

"Well, the colors are a visible embodiment of energy. They vary in hue and intensity accordin' ta the type of energy ya're sensin'. Purple is spirituality. Blue indicates a balance. Turquoise is the color of influence. Green shows healin' or growth. Yellow is joy and freedom. Orange is power. Red is malice. Pink indicates love. While dark colors are a sign of negative energy, white means death or sickness."

"Cool, so Arella can see things like anger or jealousy, not just sense someone feeling that way?" Cannon beamed at me, nodding his head and looking impressed.

Father Cillian continued, "Well now, true aura seers can perceive not only emotional energy but also physical energy."

Cannon's smile fell. "OK, you've lost me."

"What I mean is some of the more gifted seers can detect objects that are otherwise hidden from the human eye."

"So you think Arella is sensing something on Mearnaid that no one else can see, something hidden?" Cannon's eyebrows rose, waiting for the priest to affirm his statement.

Father Cillian stopped his steady gait down the rain drenched trail and turned to face us. "That I do. I believe Arella can see somethin' that has been secreted away from us for more than a century."

"The Cursing Stone?" Cannon asked. Rainwater streamed down his face, his tan skin looking pale.

"Aye, the very one."

"Now come on, how did you come to that conclusion?" It was obvious that Cannon was getting fed up with our fairy quest. "What makes you so sure it's the Cursing Stone hidden on Mearnaid and not something else, just something ordinary?"

Father Cillian looked to me. "Arella, describe the color ya saw."

I crossed my arms over my chest, the sleeves of my raincoat making an irritating squeaking noise against the din of the rain. "It was red."

"Be specific, lass."

I looked up in concentration, trying to recall the exact hue that had burned behind my lids. "It was red, kind of like the color of a garnet. It flickered like a flame, and it rippled around the edges into almost a deep purple."

The priest nodded. "Red is a materialistic color. The deeper the hue, the darker the obsession. Also, purple signifies spiritual power arising from knowledge. Together, they represent an object which is valuable because it imparts understandin' or awareness."

"You sound like an expert on auras and their seers." I eyed

the old cleric warily, suspicion settling on my shoulders like a heavy shroud.

"Aye, I've met one other seer before ya." The old cleric looked away, avoiding my eyes.

All feeling left my body except for an intense cold that seeped into my muscles and soaked my veins until I felt like I had turned to ice. I knew instantly who the other seer had been. It all made sense now; my father's managing to leave Tory, my hearing his voice, and my inheriting the gift of seeing auras was due to the fact that he was also a seer. "Why didn't you tell me before?"

"Would ya have believed before?"

I shook my head, absently flicking rainwater at Cannon's gawking face. "No, I guess I wouldn't have."

✝ ✝ ✝ ✝ ✝

We decided to go home and change out of our soaked clothing before continuing on to Mearnaid. By the time we got back to West Town, the sky had drained its reserves, but the sun remained hidden. We agreed to meet at the Tau Cross in one hour.

Aunt Fi was in her usual spot in the front room, working on another watercolor. She was humming to herself, stroking the canvas in tune to the rhythm in her head. She swayed back and forth in time, entranced by her own melody. Her back was to me, so I didn't think she noticed I was home. I could have slipped in and out again without her noticing, but the hauntingly sad tone of her song made me pause.

I took a few steps toward her, watching her work in profile. She began to sing aloud, still appearing oblivious to my presence. "*'Twas long ago when ya left me, dear, but the tears still fall in streams. I realize ya'll never return, but I see ya in my dreams.*" I watched in amazement as the wrinkles of her face seemed to smooth away with each inflection, and her eyes burned with an inner light. "*I pray each night that I may leave and join ya in the stars. But I know 'tis but a fruitless hope; I could never stray so far. So I cherish the memory of your love and wait 'til the day, when the circle of Tory will turn again and flow the other way.*"

My eyes refocused on her canvas. I recognized the subject of her painting instantly, the Tau Cross. Its stark lines against a sky of gray left me feeling empty and disappointed. I wanted to turn away. I felt almost cheated because of its ugly simplicity. I would have followed my impulse to slip away unnoticed were it not for the object in the bottom right corner, a wooden framed boat stretched over with skins, its ribs poking through the ragged covering, laying testimony to the wicked waves that had dashed it upon Tory's rocky shore. It was a scene devoid of time. My mind was pinned to the image, fretting over its significance. I wondered if Aunt Fi was painting something from Tory's past or something from my future.

"It's an old song native ta Tory."

"What?" I had forgotten about the song.

Aunt Fi turned in her seat. "It's called *An Turas Mór.*"

"Pilgrimage?"

"Aye."

"What do they mean, the words you sang?"

Aunt Fi chuckled. "Don't know. I've never really thought 'bout it."

My thoughts went back to the watercolor on the easel. "Is this another one for me?"

Aunt Fi nodded. "Aye, do ya like it?"

"Honestly, it's kind of eerie." I tried to put my finger on a reason. "The Tau Cross looks spooky, almost wicked, and the wrecked boat is disturbing."

"That's the currach of the Seven." Aunt Fi started humming again.

"The what of the who?" It was so frustrating to be constantly spoken to in riddles.

"Long ago six men and a woman were washed up on Tory's shore in a currach or small boat. St. Colm Cille ordered their bodies buried. The next morn, the body of the woman was discovered lyin' atop of the grave. She was buried again, only ta reappear. After several attempts ta bury her without success, St. Colm realized that she was a saint. She was buried as such in the nun's grave on the west side of the church. The clay from her grave is said ta be sacred. Seafarers use it as a talisman."

"So why did you paint this for me? I mean, I like the other paintings of the lighthouse and Balor's Fort, but this one and the picture of the stone that looks like some weird altar thing is just a bit strange."

Aunt Fi smiled kindly. She didn't seem at all upset at my reaction to her artwork. "They're just pictures that come ta me when I sing. The altar is Ulaí Bhríde or the Oratory of St. Brigid where holy water was collected ta relieve the pains of childbirth. It's located near St. Colm's tower."

"I don't mean to offend you, but these last two pictures are...well...creepy."

"Lass, I was just sharin' with ya a little of your Tory heritage." Aunt Fi's eyes clouded over, and her voice took on a distant tone. "When I paint, I sing, and when I sing, I see the holy places of our ancestors."

"When you sing *An Turas Mór*?"

"Aye, the song tells of the pilgrimage of the mainland sinners and the sites they visited. I've been paintin' the holy sites of Tory for ya."

"Why?"

"I don't know." The old woman shook her head, looking a bit disoriented. "I just felt ya needed ta have them ta look at. I've painted ya four, but there are three more in the song."

"What are they?"

"Cloch an Chú or Rock of the Hound, Moirsheisear, the Grave of the Seven, and Mearnaid..."

"The place where Mac Gorra was turned to stone," I said finishing her statement.

"Aye, that's right."

"Can you sing the song to me? The whole thing?"

Aunt Fi nodded and began. "*'Twas long ago when ya left me, dear, but the tears still fall in streams. I realize ya'll never return, but I see ya in my dreams. I pray each night that I may leave and join ya in the stars. But I know 'tis but a fruitless hope; I could never stray so far. So I cherish the memory of your love and wait 'til the day, when the circle of Tory will turn again and flow the other way. Walk the ring, An Turas Mór, walk the ring ta charm. Cloch na Mallacht is hidden away, on Tory ya'll see no harm. Start at Cloch Arclai, my love, traverse ta Mearnaid. Journey ta Dún Bhaloir and then on ta Cloch an Chú. Follow the path ta An Chros Tau and then ta Ulaí Bhríde . Pray at Moirsheisear for me then back ta Cloch Arclai. Walk the ring, An Turas Mór, walk the ring ta charm. Clock na Mallacht is hidden away, on Tory ya'll see no harm. Tory will see ya no harm.*" Her voice faded to a whisper. Her face settled back into its former wrinkled state, and the spark in her eyes extinguished.

My throat tightened with choked emotion. I sucked back the tears trying to escape my eyes. The worst part was I didn't know why I wanted to cry. Was it because Aunt Fi was trying to help me the only way she could, or was it because the song so plainly spelled out the fate of Tory's inhabitants.

I took my old aunt's hand in mine and forced a smile. "Thank you for the paintings, Aunt Fi. I do appreciate them."

"I know ya do, dear. And I know, too, that ya'll know what ta do with 'em."

Though I didn't understand her last statement, I nodded my head in false comprehension before excusing myself to my room.

Father Cillian, Cannon, and I met forty minutes later at the Tau Cross. It was after three o'clock in the afternoon, so there were other villagers bustling about despite the weather. Cannon was leaning his back against the crumbling base of the ancient monument, the collar of his worn leather jacket raised to protect his neck from the dampness. Father Cillian stood patiently to his left. He was all in black, including his hooded raincoat. His hands were tucked away in the openings of the opposite sleeves, making him look like a medieval monk in prayer.

"Did ya bring *The History*?" the old priest inquired from beneath his black slicker.

I exposed the old volume from beneath my raincoat then quickly replaced it to protect its pages from the rain.

"Good, we may need ta refer ta it ta help us find the Cursin' Stone. Let's be on our way then." Father Cillian led us through the narrow streets of West Town, past St. Colm's to a saturated meadow that sprawled toward Mearnaid.

As we walked, the tall, wet grass soaked through my jeans, making me wish I had worn a taller pair of boots. At least my raincoat was doing a thorough job of keeping the mist off me. The walk to Mearnaid took about twenty minutes, and by the time we arrived at the rocky edge of the cliff, my teeth were chattering.

"Mac Gorra is down there," Father Cillian said pointing over the lip.

Cannon and I both leaned over to view the stone effigy of the legendary liar. Cannon shook his head in disbelief. "I don't believe in island myths, but it sure does look like a man trying to climb the cliff."

I closed my eyes. An intense red glow flared behind my

lids. The shock of the intensity made me grab Cannon's arm. "Sorry, I almost lost my balance."

He looked startled for an instant before regaining his cocky smile. "It's OK; a lot of people are scared of heights."

I rolled my eyes and looked back across the meadow. From the direction we had come, I spied something moving in the fog. I closed my eyes, trying to read the energy. A brown and gray glow hovered in the distance, its edges burning a sulfurous yellow. "Someone's coming."

Father Cillian and Cannon turned in unison. "Who is it?" Cannon demanded.

"The energy is brown and gray, edged in a dingy yellow," I explained.

Father Cillian frowned. "Those are the colors of ill intent and anger. Quick, down over the side before he sees ya."

"What?" Cannon looked like he was about to shove the old priest. "Are you crazy? We'll fall to our death on the rocks below."

"No ya won't. There's a narrow path that leads ta Mac Gorra. Just take your time and don't make a sound. I'll get rid of whoever it is."

"It's Declan." I let my bangs hide my disappointment.

"What?" Father Cillian and Cannon gasped in unison.

"It's Declan. I've seen his aura before," I said remembering the illuminated shadows surrounding him when I had awoken in my room, disoriented from my failed escape from the island. "It's him."

Cannon growled, "I knew I hated him for some reason."

"Hurry, over the edge before he sees ya."

Cannon grumbled as he took my hand and led me to the edge. "I'll go first, just in case."

"Just in case what?" I asked, not really wanting to hear his answer, but Cannon was already descending over the edge. I mumbled a silent prayer before following him.

Father Cillian was right. There was a narrow, very narrow, path that wound down toward Mac Gorra. I chanced a look and saw Cannon steadily making his way toward the rock effigy. He was inching along like a frightened cat descending a tree, belly pressed to the wall, arms and legs spread wide. I took a deep breath and followed suit.

"Where's Arella?" It was Declan. His voice carried over the cliff in an accusing echo. I clung closer to the rock, wishing I could melt into it like Mac Gorra had.

Father Cillian's voice was remarkably calm. "Don't know. Did ya try her aunt's house?"

"Don't ya lie ta me, Father. I saw ya and Arella and Cannon leavin' town tagether."

"What business is it of yours, Declan McQuilan? I'll tutor my students as I see fit."

"Tutorin'. I don't think Father Dalbach would approve of what ya be tutorin' them in. Ya know what will happen if the charm is broken. Ya have just as much ta lose as the rest of us."

"I'll not be afraid ta meet my fate. I've lived as I should and am ready to leave this place. And, as for Father Dalbach, he answers ta me, not I ta him."

"Please," Declan's voice was pleading, "Arella can't leave. I need her. I love her, Father."

"Love? Ya know nothin' of the word. Ya be thinkin' only of yourself, Declan. Real love is selfless, not selfish. Arella doesn't belong here. Ya know that as well as I do."

Declan shouted, "No, I won't let her leave me."

As the conversation above got more and more heated, the muscles in my hands and legs began to seize up. Despite the cold, damp air, I was starting to sweat. I chanced looking down at Cannon. He had managed to reach Mac Gorra and was squeezing into a crevice next to the effigy. He would be unnoticeable from above. I decided I had to chance climbing down farther and hopefully find a similar hiding spot.

I peeled my fingers from the crevices I had burrowed them into and scooted myself slowly to the right. I felt like a shuffling old lady trying to walk without a cane. I managed to move about six feet to where the path zigzagged back to the left. I lowered myself slowly to the next rung of the trail. Reaching it, I let out a relieved breath and began inching left.

Of course, I was looking up, making sure no one was peering down at me, and I didn't see the loose rock. My foot stepped right on it and slid off the trail. The rest of my body followed. I scratched urgently at the cliff wall with my nails, desperate to find a crevice or nook to keep my balance, but the rock face slid away from me in slow motion. Gravity pulled at my body, dragging me down Mearnaid. I closed my eyes and waited for the pain.

"Arella, what the...?" Cannon's voice was full of irritation but absent of alarm. I felt his hands on me, hauling me against him.

I opened my eyes and looked around in startled disbelief. "How?"

"You can't get hurt. Remember?"

My heart was pumping a hundred miles an hour.

Cannon grabbed my hand and examined my palm. He rubbed his thumb over my skin, smearing away the dirt covering my lifeline.

I winced. The line had receded. It was now barely visible. "Looks like we're about even. About a week left."

Just then I heard Declan shout, "Get out of my way."

Cannon pulled me closer against him, trying to hide both of us in the narrow crevice. I pinched my eyes closed, afraid to look up. Cannon's blue and turquoise aura flared behind my lids, but beyond the white glowing edges, I saw red. My eyes flew open. Cannon was staring at me, a brooding smile on his lips.

"It's behind you," I exclaimed reaching behind him.

Cannon jerked his head around. "What?" he said shaking his shoulders like he was ridding himself of a spider.

"The Cursing Stone," I said with a smile.

Cannon slid as far to the side as possible and watched as I retrieved a mossy stone from an unnatural pocket in the rock behind him. The Cloch na Mallacht was unusually round, about the size of a softball. Though it was encrusted with moss and dirt, its quartz-like surface showed through where it had scraped against the rock during retrieval.

"Whoa," Cannon breathed.

I scraped at the rest of the moss hiding the stone's luster until its brilliance was no longer masked. I couldn't help gasping aloud. The stone looked like a crystal ball. Its exterior was smooth and clear, giving way to a milky interior. The inner swirls swam around a core of light which swelled under my grasp.

"You've done it, Arella." Cannon's face was colored with excitement. "You actually found the frickin' cause of our exile on this godforsaken island." Cannon grabbed my face in his hands and kissed me hard on the lips.

I pulled free, griping, "Do you mind?" I was certain, however, that my smile betrayed my excitement.

"Arella," Father Cillian called from above, "did ya find anythin'."

Cannon and I poked our heads out of our hiding spot. "Is it safe?"

"Aye, for the moment. I sent the lad down a ways ta a cave a few thousand meters ta the west. He's lookin' for ya there. Did ya find the stone?"

I held up the crystal sphere for the priest to see.

"Praise be ta God! If that ain't Cloch na Mallacht, I'm King Balor himself. Hurry back up before the lad realizes I've deceived him."

I put the Cursing Stone into an inside pocket of my raincoat and emerged from our hiding spot. I scaled Mearnaid as fast as I could shuffle my way up the winding, narrow path to the top. Cannon stayed close behind me, providing a boost or a steady hand as needed. When we reached the top of the cliff, we were wet, winded, and weary, but smiling just the same.

Chapter Eleven

So now, all we have to do is replace the stone on Cloch Arclai and the curse will be lifted?" Cannon asked.

We were all in Father Cillian's office drying ourselves by the fire, sipping black tea. Cloch na Mallacht sat in the middle of the priest's desk, its inner light glowing through the stone's milky patina. Our eyes were fixed upon the sphere while our minds were fixed upon reversing its enchantment.

"No, 'tis not that simple, I fear." Father Cillian laid Mac Gorra's *History of Tory* open to the An Turas Mór map. "Mac Gorra is tryin' ta tell us somethin' in writin' the names of the holy places backwards."

"What? That this whole island is screwed-up?" Cannon remarked, crossing his arms and leaning back in his chair. "We already know that."

"No," I said, rolling my eyes, "he's telling us that the An Turas Mór must be done in reverse, once the Cursing Stone is replaced!" I couldn't contain the excitement in my voice. It all made sense now. "Look, the names are backwards giving us the first clue. Think about it; normally, you would read left to right or in a circle clockwise. To undo what was done, you would go right to left or counterclockwise. It's all in the song Aunt Fi sang to me about An Turas Mór."

"Your Aunt sang you a song and you think you have the answer?" Cannon sneered.

I lunged at the arrogant jerk, grabbing the collar of his jacket. "Look, do you want to get out of here before our lifelines fade or what?"

"Yeah, but I don't think the answer is in a nursery rhyme

sung by a decrepit, old woman who paints in response to losing her sanity."

I tightened my hold on his collar. Father Cillian did not make a move to stop me. "If you don't want to hear me out, then leave. I'll break the curse with or without you. If you're not in, just say so."

Cannon pushed my hands away. "Yeah, I'm in. Let's hear it."

I loosened my grip. "The song Aunt Fi sang mentioned seven holy sites visited by the pilgrims of An Turas Mór. There's a line in the song that talks about the circle of Tory turning again and flowing the other way. An Turas Mór is the circle, and the part about flowing the other way means that the pilgrimage has to be done in reverse."

"What else do ya remember 'bout the song?" Father Cillian was leaning toward me, his hands flat upon his desk.

"Well, it said that Cloch na Mallacht was hidden away so now Tory would see you no harm. That's referring to the curse which doesn't allow anyone to get hurt or die on Tory."

"Does the song mention the order of the holy places ta be visited?" Father Cillian asked.

"Yeah," I said, trying to picture the pilgrimage route in my head, "it started at Cloch Arclai, the Cursing Stone's pedestal, and then went to Mearnaid. Then it goes to Balor's Fort, the Tau Cross, and a place called Brigid's altar or stone..."

Father Cillian corrected me. "Ulaí Bhríde, the Oratory of St. Brigid. That's reasonable. It's been a place of pilgrimage for women for centuries."

"The last holy spot mentioned was the Grave of the Seven."

"Moirsheisear," Father Cillian explained, "the place where the bodies of six men and one woman found dead in a curragh on Tory's shore are buried. The clay from the nun's grave is sacred. The locals believe it has powers of protection."

Cannon let out a scornful laugh. "Protect them from what? Themselves? Insanity?"

"No, the banshees comin' ta claim their souls when the curse is lifted," Father Cillian replied in a low voice full of warning. "If we undo this enchantment, every one of the villagers whose lifeline has run out will be taken ta their delayed fate by those keenin' fairies of death. Some believe the clay is a kind of talisman against meetin' this fate."

Cannon scoffed, "Sure it is."

"Once all of the holy spots are visited," I continued, "the pilgrimage must be completed by returning to Cloch Arclai."

"And turnin' Cloch na Mallacht on end," finished Father Cillian.

"So, to undo the curse, we visit the sights in the opposite order going around the island counterclockwise."

"Then what?" asked Cannon, his brows lifted in earnest concern.

"Well, we hope that will be the end of the curse. Then ya and Arella can leave. Ya can return ta your own world."

"My world? I don't know if I remember it." The sudden realization that I could at last be free caught me a little off guard. "And what about you and the others?"

"Don't ya be worrin' 'bout me. I'm ready ta move on. And the others? I think they'll realize it's for the best. Part of the joy of livin' is knowin' it's got a purpose…and an end."

"You could always try the clay," Cannon offered.

Father Cillian waved Cannon's words away. "I got no more use for charms and enchantments, don't ya know. I'm done livin' in limbo."

"OK, when do we make the circle flow the other way?" I asked.

"In two days there'll be a full moon. Ancient magic is always strongest then. We'll plan ta walk An Turas Mór then,"

Father Cillian instructed.

Cannon questioned, "And what do we do with the Cursing Stone in the meantime? You know Declan and the others will be looking for it so they can steal it away."

"We've got to keep it in a safe place," I said, stating the obvious.

Father Cillian ordered, "Arella, take it ta your aunt's cottage and hide it there."

"Are you crazy? That's the first place they'll look."

"Do ya still have those corncrakes hangin' 'round?" the old cleric asked, a scheme gleaming behind his eyes.

"Yeah?"

"I don't think they'll be lettin' anyone near ya nor near your room."

"What do you know about them?"

The priest winked, "Just a hunch, but I think they're here ta watch over ya and make sure the stone is returned. Besides, hidin' somethin' in the most obvious place is often not obvious at all."

I frowned, not quite believing him, but I took the stone anyway and hid it inside my coat before taking my copy of *The History* and leaving his office. Cannon was on my heels. "Do you mind?" I snapped.

Cannon shrugged off my irritation. "I'll just walk you home. I've got as much at stake here as you do."

I pinched a face, but he was right. We had to be careful and watch each other's backs, or neither one of us would be leaving the island. "Fine, just keep your distance. If Declan sees you walking me home, he'll know something's up."

"Hey, you're talking to the master of deceit here. How do you think I've survived this long?"

I mumbled under my breath, "Dumb luck, I'm sure."

Cannon frowned, but he didn't reply back. He probably

didn't hear my exact words, but I'm sure he got the gist of it.

We made our way quickly through West Town's dirt roads back to Aunt Fi's cottage. It was now dusk and raining once again. For once, I was glad for the dark skies and lack of sunlight. I sent up a silent prayer, hoping no one noticed us sneaking the Cursing Stone through the backstreets of An Baile Thiar. Cannon stayed well behind me, hiding the fact that he was my bodyguard. I nodded a cautious good-bye to him before letting myself in the front door of Aunt Fi's cottage.

"Arella, dear, look who's here ta pay ya a visit," Aunt Fi greeted as I closed the mudroom door behind me.

I looked up, and I'm sure my face betrayed the surprise and alarm that suddenly flared up inside of me. Father Dalbach leered at me down his pointed nose from a cozy corner spot on the parlor sofa. His dark hair was slicked back unnaturally, and his narrow chin was slanted toward me at an accusing angle. I automatically clutched the front of my coat, making sure the Cursing Stone was concealed.

"Hello, Arella," he said in a low voice sounding like an evil hiss.

Aunt Fi was bubbling like an uncorked bottle of champagne. "Arella, Father Dalbach has come ta ask ya back ta the Academy. Isn't that generous of him?"

"I...I...Thanks, but no thanks," I stuttered.

Aunt Fi's face darkened. "Now, lass, ya should be grateful he's willin' ta forgive your disobedience and let ya go back ta school."

"Your Aunt Fi's right. I'm willin' ta let ya return as long as ya promise ta give up this foolishness." He waved his hand as though he was speaking of my style of dress, but I understood what he was really referring to. I clutched the front of my coat tighter. "There's nothin' wrong with conformin' ta the rules. The good Lord smiles down on those that follow."

"Yeah, well, I'm no sheep." I waved Mac Gorra's book in the air. "If you'll excuse me, I have homework to do."

"Ah, I see ya are studyin' the book Professor McAnnals has issued ta ya. That text has been replaced with an updated version of Tory's history. When Professor McAnnals resigned, we let the new instructor choose a more appropriate book for his students."

"Professor McAnnals resigned? Why?"

"Let's just say it was a difference of opinion that made her leave."

"Where could she go? No one leaves..." I was about to say "Tory" but I caught myself and rephrased it. "No one leaves like that without saying good-bye."

"Well, she did, and I will be takin' that old text from ya and replacin' it with this one." He held out a new textbook in one hand and beckoned me to return Mac Gorra's *History of Tory* with the other. "We've found too many discrepancies in the old version."

I clutched Tory's history to my chest and shook my head stubbornly. "Thanks for the offer, but I like this version." I pushed past him roughly and stormed off to my room. I locked my door, leaned up against it, and let out a nervous sigh.

Holy crimony! Now people were going missing! I fumbled inside my jacket and pulled out Cloch na Mallacht. Its milky luster swirled before me in a mesmerizing dance of enchantment. How could such a little thing cause such big troubles?

I had to hide it, but where? Regardless of what Father Cillian said, I didn't think keeping the stone at Aunt Fi's cottage was a good idea. Father Dalbach sitting in Aunt Fi's parlor was proof of that. I decided to temporarily conceal the stone in an old soccer bag lying on the floor of my closet. I dug out the backpack and unzipped the main pocket. There I found the extra pair of socks I usually kept inside. In a fruitless effort to insulate the rock's power from those seeking it, I buried the rock between the socks. Adding the copy of Mac Gorra's *History* to its contents, I quickly returned the bag to the clutter of shoes, clothes, and dust covering my closet floor before getting myself ready for bed.

Sleep came quickly, almost as soon as my head touched the pillow. The day's climbs had worn me out, not to mention the stressful encounters with Dalbach and Declan. I remember yawning once, and then I was out.

El? El! Ya have ta wake up.

I sat bolt upright in bed. I was dripping in sweat, my night clothes sticking to me. I blinked, trying to clear away the darkness surrounding me. For a moment I couldn't remember where I was.

Then my father's voice came again. *El, they're comin'!*

Crek-crek! Crek-crek, crek-crek crek!

There was a torrent of squawks outside my window, like a fox trying to enter a hen house. The corncrakes sensed danger.

I leapt out of bed and hurried to the window. With a little caution and a lot of fear, I peeked out from behind the window shade. A thick fog had settled on the island. I couldn't see more than ten feet outside, but the nervous corncrakes fluttering just below my window were enough proof that someone or something was lurking in the mist.

I pulled on a pair of sweats over my pajamas and grabbed my soccer bag from the closet floor. I jammed my feet into a pair of boots and wrapped my coat around me. Tiptoeing to my door, I cautiously undid the lock and opened the door a crack. Everything was silent, almost too quiet. I held my breath, straining to hear my aunt snoring in the next room. I exhaled when I heard the soft vibration of air whistling over her limp palate. Opening the door wider, I went into the hall.

I kept my back to the wall as I clutched the bag with Tory's stone to my chest. I paused between each step, making sure the only sound I heard was Aunt Fi's rhythmic drone. Once inside the parlor, I headed to one of windows on the opposite side of the cottage, hoping to avoid being spotted by anyone watching the front door or my bedroom window. I climbed up on a small end table and worked open the sash. With one last look behind me, I opened the window and crawled outside.

My feet hit the ground. The sound was muffled in the wet grass. OK, now what? I had to get out of here and fast, but where?

El, the lighthouse. Remember the lighthouse? My father's voice whispered from somewhere in the recesses of my mind.

Looking left then right, I bolted away from the cottage, making a beeline for Tory Lighthouse. I didn't look back; I just ran. It wasn't far, maybe a mile and a half at most. If I didn't stop and I didn't slow down, I would be there in little over ten minutes. I put my head down and lengthened my stride.

I kept to the shadows, taking the alleys instead of the main road through town. My boots splashed through puddles and kicked up mud. If someone didn't see me, they would surely hear me, but it couldn't be helped. I sucked in more oxygen and pushed myself faster.

When I got to the edge of town, I stopped to catch my breath behind an old warehouse. From the smell surrounding it, I could only guess what byproduct of the day's catch it stored: fish oil? fish eggs? guts? I sucked in a putrid lungful of air and surveyed the remainder of my route. The rest of the way to Tory Light was across open ground. The only cover I could hope for was the murky night. I tucked the bag with the stone under my arm and darted into the open.

Pushing away the panic, I ran fast and hard. My breath pulled in and out like the sound of a steam engine. I leaned into the salty air and fixed my eyes on the faint outline of the light's tower. If I could make it to the lighthouse, I would be safe. Why I knew this I didn't know, but just the same, I was sure.

My heart beat faster, and my legs pumped harder. The damp air whipped past me, making my skin bead with moisture and my hair tangle behind me. Tripping and splashing over rocks, puddles, and tufts of grass, I neared Tory Lighthouse without incident. I chanced a look behind me, and that's when I saw what I had expected all along.

A dark figure raced after me. It was tall and broad in the shoulders. From its quick and steady gait, I knew right away it was Declan. Crap!

I clutched the bag tighter and kicked my speed up a notch. I could outrun him. His stride was longer, but I was quicker. The problem was there was no place to go. Even if the lighthouse tower wasn't locked, Declan would surely find me hiding inside, and then it would all be over. He'd find the stone, and Cannon and I would be stuck on Tory forever.

"Damn you, Declan McQuilan!" I seethed between gritted teeth. Then I realized he already was. I put my head down and pushed my legs faster.

Tory Lighthouse loomed in front of me. It was a gaping shadow against the void of night. The nearly full moon was veiled behind a thick layer of black clouds which prevented most of its light from illuminating the scene. It looked like something out of a cheap horror film, and I caught myself thinking I was the dumb girl who would soon find she was the next victim of the insane maniac on the loose. I raced straight for the base of the light tower, my lungs pumping like the bellows of a furnace.

"Arella, why are ya runnin'? I need ta talk ta ya!" Declan's call was so loud that it sounded like he was just a few feet behind me. My stomach churned.

I raced around the base of the lighthouse looking for a place to hide. I found the door leading into the tower and gave the handle a quick jiggle. Locked!

I didn't look to see where Declan was. There wasn't time. I just ran. I stumbled and caught myself twice in the next fifty yards. I had a feeling the next trip would land me face first in the dirt, so I slowed a bit. After another twenty yards the footing suddenly seemed more stable, and I realized I was on a narrow gravel path. Where it led I hadn't a clue, but I took advantage of the fast track and let loose the last of my speed.

Declan screamed behind me, "El, stop! Don't ya go any farther!" His voice shook with terror.

I faltered, but I didn't stop. Ahead was a black iron gate, bent against its hinges, banging open and closed in the wind. Beyond the gate, an army of mossy stones leaned into formation…headstones. Gravel ground under my feet as I slid to a stop. I turned to face Declan, my back against the gate.

"El, don't go in there," Declan warned, his face pale and distraught.

I swallowed hard, forcing down my fear. I tucked the bag with Tory's stone behind my back with one hand and grabbed the gate with my other. "Why not, Declan?"

He winced like my move pained him. "Please, El, don't enter the gate."

"Why should I do anything you ask?" I was stalling, trying to remember if I had read anything about the graveyard in Mac Gorra's *History* that would make Declan not want me to enter.

Declan held out his hand and stepped toward me. He forced a weak smile. "I can't lose ya, El. I can't go on if ya leave me. Don't ya want ta stay with me? Don't ya love me, El?"

"I…I…" My head began to swim. I knew I should tell him to step off, but the words wouldn't come. He looked frail, like my next words could shatter him to pieces. I fought against the urge to reach out to him though my heart throbbed like it would puncture my chest.

Then he gave me his crooked smile. I felt myself waver. He took a step toward me, and my knees liquefied. Declan caught me in his arms and pulled me toward him. "We can be tagether forever. We'll never be parted, El. Our love will be eternal." His whisper caressed my cheek. I closed my eyes in anticipation of his kiss.

Dark shadows coalesced behind my eyelids. Muddy swirls of gloom swam through a gray fog edged in a sulfur haze. Negativity, depression, pain, fear, and anger crept closer, but I was paralyzed.

I was no longer concerned about the stone. I didn't care about leaving Tory. I didn't think about breaking the curse. In that moment, my only thought was of Declan McQuilan, and how I could be with him forever.

"Declan, stop!" chimed a familiar, high-pitched voice.

My wits slammed back to me. I opened my eyes and gasped for breath. Brigid Dunn was standing just six feet to the left. Her lips were puckered into an agitated bow, and her hands were clenched on her hips. Her braid flicked from side to side as she looked from Declan to me and back again. Her gray eyes caught the veiled light of the moon. They shined full of anger like a caged animal.

Declan's face creased with fury. "Brigid, go home and leave me be."

"No," Brigid replied, planting her feet firmly. "I know what you're doin' and it's wrong. Let Arella go. Don't condemn her ta this place."

What? I looked from one to the other in complete confusion. Was Brigid actually trying to help me?

Declan turned his attention away from me and took a step toward Brigid. His hands were balled into fists, and his shoulders were arched forward in rage. "Ya mind your own affairs and leave us be."

Declan towered over the girl like a bear ready to attack, but Brigid stood her ground.

I was in shock. Brigid had struck me as a social strategist, not a champion of righteousness, but here she was standing against Declan instead of trying to schmooze.

"Ya don't need to keep her here, Declan. Ya don't need her." Brigid extended one of her hands toward Declan, her fingers shaking with emotion.

Now I understood. She wanted me to leave. She wanted me out of the picture. If I were gone, Declan would be all hers. Keeping my eyes on the two of them, I backed silently through the gate and into the cemetery.

"She has the Cursin' Stone, Brigid." Declan's voice betrayed his agony. "She'll undo us all."

"I don't care," Brigid cried. "Let her go."

Declan moved toward the shaking girl, an evil scowl rippling across his features.

"Run, Arella!" Brigid screamed as she lunged at Declan and knocked him on his back.

I took off at a full sprint. Sailing over toppled monuments and rounding mossy headstones, I raced blindly through the burial ground, the hidden Tory stone tucked tightly under my arm, my raincoat flapping loosely at my sides. I felt like a deranged spirit looking for someone to haunt.

The graveyard was a blur of shadows in the veiled moonlight, but after a few minutes, I found myself on the opposite end of the cemetery. I hung my head to my knees and gulped in a lungful of air. My breathing slowed. I scanned the area, looking for any sign of Declan. I was alone. Should I hop the fence and find Father Cillian, or should I just wait out the rest of the night inside the protection of the rod iron fence?

A gnarled old oak caught my attention. Its exposed roots clung desperately to the rocky soil while its knotted branches reached pleadingly toward the murky sky. I instinctively walked toward it, wanting to lay a hand on the rough bark. I closed my eyes. Orange and green light radiated in front of my closed lids. Power and growth. The oak was a monument to life in this place of death.

I stepped toward the light, and I nearly tripped. Beneath the boughs of the ancient tree was an old limestone grave marker. It leaned awkwardly in the damp ground, looking like the next stiff breeze would topple it. I knelt down trying to read the faded inscription. The letters were obscured by moss and dirt. I raked my fingers over the stone's patina, trying to uncover the name. Two letters emerged: D and Q.

I worked my fingers faster, rubbing and scraping. Another letter surfaced: L. Spurred on by a combination of curiosity and fear, I chafed the stone harder. An M appeared. I started to sweat. I used the lining of my coat to buff off the rest of the dirt. When the entire inscription materialized, I sat back on my heels and let an agonized moan escape my lips. The stone's writing was horrifyingly clear: DECLAN MCQUILAN 1866-1884.

Tears streamed down my cheeks. I had known it was true, but I had held onto the hope that somehow the magic of Tory would keep me from fully realizing this awful reality. I shook my head against the pain. A sinister chill filled me. If the An Turas Mór enchantment was not broken soon, a stone with my name would soon join the others. I reached into my backpack to reassure myself that I still had the Cursing Stone. The rock was cold and hard under my fingertips, a harsh reminder that I couldn't allow myself to fail.

"Arella." Declan approached through the swirling fog, holding out his hands in surrender. "I want ta explain. Please, listen ta me."

Brigid clung to his arm, trying to pull him away. "No, Arella, go." Her voice was hoarse with desperation.

I scrambled to my feet, swaying a bit with indecision. "I already know, Declan," I choked out between tortured sobs.

"But do ya know why I did it? Do ya know why I would curse my homeland, my neighbors, and myself?"

"Declan, stop!" Brigid's voice pitched higher in her anxiety.

"No, I'm tired of hidin' it. Arella, I cursed Tory and all on it ta save it. And I was afraid ta die with such sins on my head."

"What sins?" I knew I should run, but my feet had become rooted firmly in the grass.

"I used the Cursin' Stone ta conjure a storm. It was long, long ago. The year was 1884." He paused, obviously looking for my reaction to the date. When I didn't give him one, he continued, "I did it ta cause the HMS Wasp ta crash upon the rocks. I saw the ship, and I knew it was comin' ta collect taxes from the island. We were barely gettin' by, El. The children were beggin' on the docks for food. The fishermen were sellin' their boats ta feed their families. Homes were bein' abandoned. Somethin' had ta be done, or we would've all starved ta death.

"When I saw the ship caught in the wind and waves I'd created with the Tory Stone, I raced ta the top of Tory Light and doused its beacon and waited for the vessel ta flounder upon the rocks. The HMS sunk. There were no survivors."

"You killed all those people?" I was stunned by the matter-of-fact way he told his tale.

Declan's face darkened. His voice became angry and defensive. "After the shipwreck, I was ashamed of what I'd done. I hid the Cursin' Stone. I didn't realize it 'til some time later, but I had trapped Tory and all the islanders in time by usin' the stone."

I shook my head, trying to wrap it around what Declan was

saying. "But, you're dead." I pointed to his headstone.

He nodded as he held his palms out for my scrutiny. "My gravestone marks the year my body died, but my soul still remains. The guilt eats at me, El. I tried ta throw myself from the Wishin' Stone prayin' ta die, but I guess ya can't undo a curse with a wish."

"Oh, Declan!" The words erupted from my chest as an anguished sob.

"I can never let the curse be undone and face the consequences of my actions. Give me the stone, Arella. If ya undo the curse, I'll be damned forever for both murder and suicide."

I shivered at his words. "No, Declan, I can't." I put the bag with the stone behind my back, as if that would protect it.

Brigid dragged on Declan's arm. "Declan, let her go!"

"I can't! I'll be damned ta hell." Declan pushed Brigid aside and lunged at me.

"You already are!" I jumped back, tripping over one of the anonymous tombstones. I fell flat on my back into a tangle of weeds. My breath swooshed out of me, and I felt like I was going to pass out.

Declan was suddenly looming over me, his handsome face horribly twisted in anger. I could hear Brigid whimpering nearby. Oh, God, the stone! Where was it? I turned and saw my soccer bag lying just a foot away. I inched my fingers toward it, hoping Declan wouldn't notice.

"Sorry, El." Declan stepped on my hand. "I can't let ya do that." He snatched up the bag and dug inside. His hand emerged, holding the Tory Stone. Discarding the bag, he knelt down on my arms and leaned his face close to mine, so close I could feel his icy breath on my face. He gripped my chin with a cold hand and turned my face toward the swirling stone. "Truly I could not give either one of ya up, but ta lose ya both would break my heart." The back of his hand caressed my cheek. I jerked my face away. He laughed loudly then released my arms and stood.

I slowly pulled myself to my feet. The stone pulsed in Declan's hand. So this was it? I was beat, and Declan had won.

"Don't look so sad, El. I'll take care of ya. We'll be happy tagether." His empty words rattled through my brain like chains of incarceration. "I love ya, Arella, and now we can be tagether forever."

My head slumped forward. The breath was sucked out of me. I looked at my palms. Could I even see my lifeline anymore? I already felt dead, so I might as well be.

Just then, a familiar voice cut through the churning fog. "Give it back to her."

Declan turned away from me toward the figure emerging from an eddy of mist. "Oh, come on, Cannon. Your lifeline must've run out by now. Ya have just as much ta lose as the rest of us," Declan waved to Brigid, including her in the stakes, "if Arella undoes the curse."

My voice came back to me. "No, he still has a chance."

"Really? Now that's interestin'." Declan stepped toward Cannon. "I would've thought our last encounter was enough ta do ya in."

"No," Cannon answered, his hands knotting in fists. "I've got a little life left in me yet."

"Well, we'll have ta take care of that," Declan said as he sent his fist straight into Cannon's gut.

Cannon fell to the ground, hitting his head against a broken tombstone. Brigid screamed, launching herself at Declan. The two of them toppled onto Cannon, and the threesome immediately became an indistinguishable tangle of flailing arms and legs. In the mayhem, the Cursing Stone rolled free of Declan's grip. And no one seemed to notice, but me.

The Tory Stone came to rest on a pile of dry grass. The energy within it pulsed wildly, seemingly agitated by the jostling. Before the chaos could be sorted out, I snatched the stone and took off running.

This time I vaulted over the grave markers like I had wings, no tripping, no floundering. I made it to the fence, and still no one was after me. I shoved the Cursing Stone into my pocket and... Crap! Where was my pack? Mac Gorra's *History* was still inside. I couldn't leave it.

I retraced my steps, keeping one eye on the wrestling match still raging between Cannon and Declan while searching for my soccer bag with the other. As each second ticked away, I knew my chance for escape was dwindling.

After several fruitless seconds of searching, I couldn't delay any longer. With one last sweep of the area, I gave up the search and shimmied up one side of the fence and dropped to the ground on the other. I bolted away from the cemetery like a bat out of hell, which wasn't too far from the truth.

Chapter Twelve

I ran blindly into the darkness without a destination in mind. I wanted to get as far away from Declan and the cemetery as possible, and I didn't really care where I ended up. I stayed away from the road, knowing I had less of a chance running into someone if I avoided going back into West Town.

I sloshed across a sodden field of tall weeds and wild grasses. At one time it had probably been plowed ground, but after years of neglect, it had reverted back to raw countryside. I stumbled upon an abandoned, rusty plow, a grim reminder of how Tory's inhabitants had turned their backs on the passing of time.

The ground became spongier under my feet. My legs felt like lead weights. Exhaustion finally got the better of me. I sank to my knees, my strength gone and my will spent. I fought to keep my flickering eyelids from closing all the way, but in the end I lost the battle and gave in to sleep.

El, wake up! El, listen ta me!

Yellow light forced away the darkness. I felt warm and protected, like a down comforter had been wrapped around me. I nestled deeper into the sweet oblivion of sleep.

Arella Cline, can ya hear me?

Let me be. I'm tired.

Then, a shadow crossed into the yellow light, a familiar shadow of a man. He reached his hand toward me. I resisted the urge to reach for it at first. I wanted the peace and quiet of being asleep, but the man was persistent.

El, take my hand.

Reluctantly, I reached out to the apparition. The presence

grew, pushing away the yellow light until the silhouette dissolved into a flock of fluttering black shadows that scattered then disappeared.

Crek-crek-crek-crek-crek.

"Arella, wake yourself."

My eyes opened. I couldn't focus at first. Everything was a blur of color and light. After blinking several times, the figure came into focus. Father Cillian's plump face and bulbous nose materialized before me, a silly grin stretching from one ear to the other.

"Ya're the most stubborn lass I've ever met. And it's a good thing, too." He grabbed my arm and pulled me to my feet.

"How did you find me?" I asked, rubbing my eyes.

The chubby cleric pointed to several corncrakes that had settled in the grass nearby. "Those birds are never far from where ya are."

"What happened?"

"Well, it appears that ya managed ta keep yourself alive for one more day," the priest said, examining my palms.

"But where are Cannon and Brigid?"

"Well, ya're just full of questions now, aren't ya? Cannon is in my office, safely sleepin'. However, I know nothin' of the whereabouts of Brigid Dunn. Why do ya ask?"

Trying to shake off the last of the sleep clouding my brain, I answered, "She...she helped me last night."

"Really? Now that's surprisin'."

I rubbed the last of the sleep from my eyes then felt my pockets for the Cursing Stone. I retrieved the crystal from inside my coat. The lustrous sphere throbbed with energy. I could feel the warmth of its power swelling from its core.

Remembering the events of last night's escape, disappointment suddenly overshadowed the joy. *The History of Tory* was lost. I had left it somewhere in the graveyard. "Father,

I think Declan has the original copy of Mac Gorra's *History*. I'm sorry, but I lost it."

"What do ya mean?" His voice was soft, free of anger. "It's right there." He pointed to the ground.

I turned abruptly. Sure enough, my soccer backpack lay open on the wet grass, my copy of Tory's history peeking out of it. I picked up the book, trying to remember last night's events clearly. Hadn't I scaled the wrought iron fence without the bag? "I don't understand. I thought it was lost."

"Perhaps your guardian angel returned it ta ya," Father Cillian said with a wink. "Now, let's get ya back ta St. Colm's before Declan and Father Dalbach catch up ta us."

✞ ✞ ✞ ✞ ✞

When we arrived in the priest's office, Cannon was sleeping on a wooden pew situated next to the fireplace. The hearth glowed softly with the remnants of a fire.

The boy's knees were curled to his chest, his body awkwardly positioned on its side. His amber hair was tousled and dark with sweat. His chin was shadowed with stubble. His face, however, looked free of pain. Peace had settled over his features, smoothing away the remnants of last night's confrontation. His arms were also relaxed, sprawled loosely about. One was flung over his head. The other hung limply to the ground.

My eyes zeroed in on his open palms. Oh, no! My breath caught in my chest. I couldn't see either one of his lifelines. "Cannon, oh, Cannon!" I grabbed his hands to inspect them closer. "It was Declan's punch. Oh, I'm so sorry."

"Arella," Cannon said as he sat up, "what are you talking about?" He pushed me away gently while yawning.

"Your hands!" was all I could manage.

Father Cillian laid a soothing hand on each of our shoulders. "Now, now, all is not lost, yet. He still has a wee bit of a lifeline on both hands. Look." The priest pointed to two faint red dots on either of Cannon's palms. "Yet, there is a bit of a rub. I don't think they'll remain 'til tamorrow night. We'll have ta walk the An Turas Mór tonight, or it'll be too late for the lad."

I shook my head, not believing our bad luck. "I thought we had to wait for the full moon."

"Well, the ancient magic is always strongest under a full moon, but I'm afraid we'll have ta chance it a bit early. I pray we'll be forgiven this small indiscretion."

"So tonight's the night then." Cannon ran his hand through his messy hair, making it stand up on end. "I may finally get the chance to go home."

I closed my eyes. Cannon's aura burned yellow with joy. Traces of pink ebbed in and out of his core. The edges of his inner energy, however, flared white. Death was closing in. I squeezed my eyes tighter, trying to keep the tears from escaping. If Cannon didn't go home tonight, he never would.

We stayed sequestered in Father Cillian's office for the rest of the day, pouring over *The History*, making sure we knew exactly how to perform the ritual that would undo the curse. As far as we could tell, the enchantment would be undone if a number of penitents, which we were, followed the original route in reverse. We would begin at Cloch Arclai shortly after dark by replacing the Cursing Stone on its original pedestal. Then we would proceed to each of the holy spots following a counterclockwise path, leaving a small stone and offering a prayer. Upon returning to Cloch Arclai, we would turn the Cursing Stone upside down, and the absolution would then be complete.

"Ancient magic waxes and wanes with the moon," Father Cillian explained. "We must finish when the magic is strongest, especially since we are performin' the ritual a night earlier than planned. The entire ritual must be completed as close ta midnight as possible without goin' past."

"Just like Cinderella, aye, Father?" Cannon joked.

We all chuckled at the comment, but the truth of Cannon's statement soon struck us silent. Would any of this hocus-pocus really work? Or was it all just a charade we were willing to play out to keep ourselves from believing in an even more bizarre reality?

Cinderella's tale ended in happily ever after. Would mine? Perhaps the fairytale I was stuck in would be more like one of the Grimm Brothers' stories, just another macabre anecdote that ended in a gruesome finale. Cinderella had a fairy godmother to look after her and make sure she escaped her old miserable existence. Who would come to my rescue?

My heart answered my own question before my mind had time to even consider the candidates. Aunt Fi was as close to a fairy godmother as any. She had taken me in and given me a family when I thought I had none left. She had comforted me with kind words and gifts of her talent, and in the end, she had even given me the key to escaping Tory.

I turned to Father Cillian. "How long do we have?"

"A few hours."

"There's something I have to take care of," I said shrugging on my jacket and heading to the door.

Cannon stood up trying to get between me and the exit. "Arella, you can't chance going out there and having Declan or Dalbach find you."

"Listen." I glared at Cannon, waving an angry finger in his face. "I have to say good-bye to Aunt Fi. I can't just leave without telling her..." I gulped at the lump forming in my throat. "...without telling her I love her, and I'll miss her. I can't face another good-bye without closure."

"Fine, fine," Cannon agreed, "but I'm coming with you to make sure you make it to Cloch Arclai on time. Father Cillian can meet us there with the stone at dusk."

The old priest nodded. "Agreed. But stick tagether, they'll be expectin' one of ya ta be carryin' the Tory stone. They know their time is runnin' out and will be desperate ta stop us."

"Don't worry about us; just get yourself and the stone to Cloch Arclai. We'll be waiting." Cannon waved to the priest and ushered me out the door.

Classes were long over at St. Colm's, so the halls were empty. The closest exit was through the main hall. We hurried along, the squeaking of our rubber boots amplified by the silence.

"Can I help ya, now?" It was the thick-spectacled registrar.

"Uh, no ma'am," I blurted out. We just finished meeting with Father Cillian. We're on our way out."

She looked me up and down, her coke-bottle eyes settling on my hands. "I can see ya still haven't reviewed the dress code portion of your handbook."

I glanced down at my fingernails. They looked ragged, most of the black polish was chipped away from my recent rock climbing excursion. "Um, I'll take care of that as soon as I get home. Thanks for the reminder." Cannon and I rushed out, not looking back.

We skirted through the drizzle, taking the backstreets and alleys to Aunt Fi's cottage. Constantly glancing back, afraid that Cannon or Dalbach would sneak up on us, we doubled our pace. The town, however, appeared deserted. Once at the cottage, Cannon followed me into the mudroom, but he graciously refused to come inside the house. Aunt Fi was in the parlor, sitting silently in front of a blank canvas when we arrived.

"You're not humming," I said, clicking the door to the

mudroom shut behind me.

"Oh, I don't feel the urge, I s'pose."

"Why are you crying?" I asked. Aunt Fi's eyes were glassy with tears. I hadn't thought she knew about our plan.

Aunt Fi smiled sadly; her lips showed pale beneath the painted-on color. She took my hand in both of hers. Her touch was cold but soothing. "I want ya ta know that I was happy ta have ya in my house, lass. Ya were a comfort and a joy."

"Aunt Fi." I hugged her tightly, and the tears began to fall. "I'll never forget your kindness. Thank you for all of the paintings. And thank you for…for everything."

"I have one more," she said, gently pulling away from my embrace. "I have one more paintin' for ya." She dug in her pocket and pulled out a silver chain with a T-shaped charm dangling from it. The chain was thick and coarsely made; the metal was tarnished with age. She placed the necklace in my hand and gently closed my fingers over it.

I unfolded my hand. "The Tau Cross!"

"It's a prayer box."

I shook my head not understanding.

"Ya have ta open it, don't ya know."

My fingers fumbled with the latch. Inside was a small slip of parchment. I carefully unfolded the tiny piece of vellum. "Oh, Aunt Fi!" Bright yellows and bold oranges radiated from the miniature piece of art. It was a painting of a sunrise.

"It's a picture of dawn, a reminder that each day is a new beginnin'. And the prayer box was a gift from your father. He gave it ta me before he left Tory. I want ya ta have it."

My eyes blurred. Dad had made it out of Tory, and now I would, too. My thoughts turned to Aunt Fi. Would she be able to endure being left behind once again? I closed my eyes. Aunt Fi's aura burned bright. Waves of blue, purple, and pink rippled around her, a sea of balanced spirituality underlined by the radiant glow that only love can give.

I threw my arms around her shoulders and whispered, "Thank you."

Aunt Fi gently brought me to arms length. "Ya're welcome, lass. Now go quickly."

I nodded, smearing away my tears with the back of my hand. I slipped my father's charm over my head and tucked it away beneath my shirt. The cold metal sent a shiver over my skin. Was the tremor a warning of things to come?

"Arella, we better roll," Cannon said, sticking his head around the mudroom door.

I left the parlor as Aunt Fi began to sing the song of An Turas Mór. "*'Twas long ago when ya left me, dear, but the tears still fall in streams. I realize ya'll never return, but I see ya in my dreams. I pray each night that I may leave and join ya in the stars. But I know 'tis but a fruitless hope; I could never stray so far...*"

I stifled the sobs rising in my throat. "Yeah, let's roll."

The click of the blue door closing behind me for the last time echoed in my head despite the fact that the damp air should have muffled all sound. I didn't look back; I couldn't. Cannon didn't say anything, though I knew he was trying to read my face in the dark. Finally, he stopped looking at me, probably realizing he'd never know what I was really thinking.

We traveled the distance to Cloch Arclai in nervous silence. Cannon twitched his head back and forth every few seconds, no doubt expecting Declan around every corner, but there was no one. That made me even more nervous. Where were Declan and Dalbach? Why weren't they stalking us?

When Tory's rocky shore came into view and I could see the ancient pedestal of Cloch na Mallacht looming against the churning night sky, I realized why no one was pursuing us. Declan and Dalbach were leaning against the pedestal, awaiting our arrival. With them were three others. I recognized the boys from the soccer game--Connor, Keenan, and Bryce.

"Who invited them," Cannon exclaimed through gritted teeth.

"We have to face them. We have to put the Cursing Stone back on the pedestal to start the ritual." Just then I remembered Father Cillian. "Once Father gets here with the stone."

"You mean, if he gets here. Declan's probably already stolen the Tory Stone and locked up Father Cillian somewhere. We're done."

"No, look." I pointed to five figures approaching from the right. A beam of moonlight illuminated their forms like actors moving onstage. Father Cillian's pear-shaped body led the way.

"Well, I'll be damned."

"Let's hope not," I said, shooting Cannon an irritated look for his choice of words. I instantly forgot my annoyance, however, when I saw who the other figures were. Behind Father Cillian I recognized Brigid Dunn's lithe form and braided ponytail. Beside her was Colin Donland, his red hair tousled and standing on end like some fiend resurrected from purgatory. Eoin O'Riley, St. Colm's Gaelic professor, followed looking exactly like the leprechaun I suspected he was. Behind them all, Professor McAnnals came, waving her cane with the wrath of a wizard's staff.

Cannon and I jogged toward the gathering.

"Declan McQuilan and Father Dalbach, we've come here ta end the curse of An Turas Mór. Stand down or be put down." Father Cillian's face was severely lined by the gravity of his words.

"Don't flatter yourself, old man," Declan countered. "Ya and your ragtag clan of do-gooders can't stop us from reclaimin' the stone. Might as well hand it over before ya regret it."

"Declan, we're putting things right." I said, trying to make him see that we were justified in our cause. "This curse can't go on."

His eyes fixed on mine, and I felt the pull of his being. "El, I tried ta make ya see things my way, but ya're just too hardheaded. Ya'll eventually get used ta Tory and learn ta love it. Just like ya'll learn ta love me."

I shook my head, pulling myself free of his allure. "Yeah, I don't think so. I don't think I can love someone who only thinks of himself."

"El, I love ya, don't ya see that? I want us ta be tagether. I'm thinking of us."

Declan's face was twisted in pain, but I ignored the urge to put my arms around him and forgive all he had done. "I want to go home," I insisted.

"Ya can't. I won't let ya." His face was suddenly ugly with smugness.

"It's not up to you anymore," Cannon said.

Father Cillian approached the pedestal. His hands were tucked beneath his billowing sleeves. He was dressed in his black vestments, and his face was serious to the point of frightening. His white hair stood out around his head in a crown of windblown wisps. In the darkness, he appeared as a wraith floating above the ground, the sight of which sent a ripple of chills along my spine.

I closed my eyes to read his aura. Turquoise and orange flames flared from his form, the colors of influence and power. I smiled to myself; he was ready for the fight.

Reaching under his robes, he withdrew Cloch na Mallacht. "Move aside, lad."

Declan puffed out his chest and stepped toward the priest. "Ya'll have ta make me."

Father Dalbach and the three young soccer players stepped

forward as one, signaling allegiance to their leader, Declan, without a word. Father Cillian stood his ground, holding the Cursing Stone firmly in front of him. His supporters moved to his side, joining the priest in blatant defiance of the threat.

"Declan, this is wrong." Brigid's voice bubbled high with tension. "What ya've done is unnatural. How long are we ta go on like this?"

Colin chimed in, "Yeah, Dec, it's enough."

Declan turned on Colin like a rabid dog. "Even ya betray me now. Are ya so swayed by a pretty face that ya would turn your back on your best friend."

"This isn't right what ya do." Colin hung his head remorsefully before taking a step back behind the professors.

"Enough!" Declan's face burned with fury. "Give it ta me." He lunged for Father Cillian and the stone.

The old priest stepped back, but Declan was on him, quick as a cat on a mouse. The cleric went down, and Declan went with him. Colin jumped on Declan, attempting to pull him off. Soon Connor, Kennan, and Bryce joined in. Punches flew. Profanity overflowed, and before I knew it, everyone was in the throes of an out and out brawl.

In the midst of all the confusion, the Cursing Stone rolled away unnoticed, unnoticed by everyone but me. I pounced on the magical swirling sphere just as it slid from under Colin's grappling form. It spun in a dizzying circle before it came to rest at the base of the pedestal. I cradled it in my hand like it was a precious jewel. Precious it was, but far more valuable than any jewel. In my hand, I held my very life.

The seat of the Cursing Stone was obvious. In the center of Cloch Arclai was a perfectly sized indentation the exact size of the stone. With shaking fingers, I matched the sphere to the hole. Like metal to a magnet, the crystal orb affixed itself to the pedestal.

A wave of blue light flexed across the night like a swell of visible energy. The entire sky rippled, bowing and flexing like a sheet of cellophane. It looked like a picture I had seen once in a book of the aurora borealis, but on a much larger and more impressive scale. There was a weird, high-pitched sound that accompanied the show of lights. It resonated through the air like the irritating whine of a child's toy whistle. I closed my eyes and held my ears, protecting myself from the apocalypse.

"Arella, let's go." Cannon pulled me away from the pedestal.

The others were cowering from the lights, too afraid to notice us.

"But the Tory Stone!" I exclaimed.

"It's been joined to its base. It can't be removed now until the An Turas Mór is completed. Let's go before Declan tries to stop us."

I nodded and took his outstretched hand. We ran along the island's southern shore heading to the next holy site on the An Turas Mór. Moirsheisear, the Grave of the Seven.

Chapter Thirteen

"What...do...we do...now?" I gasped, putting my hands on my knees, trying to catch my breath. We were on the outskirts of West Town, and the streets looked empty. I couldn't help thinking we were headed right into an ambush.

Cannon looked around as if he had read my thoughts. "Well, Father said we say a prayer and leave a rock at each of the sites." He bent down, grabbing a smooth pebble from the road. "Let's go inside the chapel." He tossed the pebble in the air and caught it in his hand before moving toward the small clapboard structure marking the Grave of the Seven.

I followed Cannon into the unlocked oratory. The building was no bigger than a shed. A single candle lit the interior, flickering distorted shadows on the whitewashed walls. There was an altar, plain and bare except for a simple wooden cross in the shape of a T resting in the middle of it. We approached the altar and knelt before it.

"What do we say?" I asked, afraid the wrong words would undo all we had already done.

"I don't know," Cannon answered as he stared at the cross.

Closing my eyes, I concentrated on the altar. Radiant golden light burned through the darkness of my eyelids.

El, talk ta me. I know ya can hear me.

"Daddy? Help me get home," I whispered.

"Well," Cannon cut in, "those aren't the words I would've used, but they're fitting I guess." He put the stone he had picked up from the road on the altar and helped me to my feet.

"Ulaí Bhríde is next," I said, "the Oratory of St. Brigid."

Cannon nodded and escorted me outside. We started

toward the road, but I pulled back when I remembered what Aunt Fi had said about the clay from the nun's grave. "Wait here. I'll just be a minute."

Cannon's face twisted, showing his reluctance to delay. "Arella, we have to hurry."

"I know," I said running back toward the chapel, "I'll be quick."

I wasn't sure where to look, but a white stone marker on the west side of the building drew my attention. There was no inscription on it, just an etching of the Tau Cross. This had to be it. I plunged my fingers into the moist ground surrounding the shrine. The soil was sticky and pliable, like the clay we had used in art class to make ashtrays and flowerpots. I shoved two large clods of the stuff in my coat pockets and returned to where Cannon was waiting.

"St. Brigid's oratory isn't far. Come on." Cannon took off running.

We sprinted for a couple of blocks until we came to the Round Tower. I remembered that McGorra's *History* stated that it had been part of St. Colm's monastery in the sixth century. It was an impressive structure despite the fact that over time the top half of it had crumbled away, probably eroded by the unrelenting Tory rain.

"It's just behind the tower. Most people miss it because it just looks like a hunk of rock," Cannon explained.

I walked behind the Round Tower. The air was heavy with moisture, but the moon's light cut through the dampness coming to rest on the stone altar. It was a large gray rectangle, smoothed by time. On the top were three wells, holy water fonts. Closing my eyes, I read its energy. Blue light emanated from the altar, the same kind of blue I remembered the skies back home as being. Clear, beautiful, limitless. And bordering the blue light was a glimmer of emerald green. Energy with the power to heal.

I opened my eyes. Something shimmered in the three fonts—water. Holy water? No, rainwater, but I dipped my fingers in it just the same. I made the sign of the cross, blessing myself out loud, hoping the words would suffice as a prayer.

"Don't forget the rock," Declan reminded.

I nodded as I picked up a granite chip and placed it on the altar. I turned to leave.

Just then there was an abrupt movement in my peripheral vision. Without thinking, I gripped Cannon's arm. I didn't realize that my nails were digging into his skin until he protested loudly, "Hey, what are you doing? That hurts!"

"You're feeling pain!" I gasped.

Cannon's gaze swept the area. His voice was shaky. "Yeah, we better move."

An Chros Tau, the Tau Cross, was our next stop on the pilgrimage. We sneaked through town, staying out of the road, our backs against the buildings, our eyes anxiously darting back and forth. I didn't see anyone following us, which made me even more fearful. If I'm gonna get attacked, I'd rather see it coming.

An Chros Tau stood on a two tier dais of hewn granite. The edges of the individual blocks of stone had been sanded away by time into a smooth, fissureless platform. Silhouetted against the night sky, it was a petrified symbol of man's attempt at understanding the divine, just another bitter reminder that, as humans, we always fall short, like the cross that looks like a T.

I stepped toward the monument. Footsteps crunched in the gravel behind me. I assumed it was Cannon, so I ignored the sound and continued toward the cross. A searing pain stopped me short. My hand flew to my head as I cried out in agony. The hurt cut through my left temple and shot over to my right, sending a debilitating jolt of pain through my entire body.

El, I know ya can hear me. Open your eyes.

"Arella?" Cannon had me under the arms. I was slumped against him, his arms supporting all of my weight.

I cried out again, like a wounded animal. Another shockwave of pain wracked my brain, sending me to my knees.

"What's the matter, Arella?" Cannon hunched over me as he helped me sit on the ground. His face was pale, beaded with moisture. His eyes darted back and forth over my face.

I whispered, afraid to make the confession, "I…felt… pain."

Cannon's eyes widened. Behind him, a shadowy figure

drifted in and out of the darkness, looking like it was trying to decide whether or not to approach. Cannon followed my gaze. "What are you looking at?"

"Don't you see it?"

Cannon shook his head and hurried me to my feet. "Come on, Arella. We gotta say a prayer and leave a rock fast. I don't know what's going on, but it can't be good." With his arm around my shoulders, Cannon propped me up in front of the Tau Cross. He shoved a stone in my hand and made the sign of the cross with his free arm.

I limply tossed the stone onto the dais and mumbled, "Come, Holy Spirit, fill the hearts of your faithful and kindle in them the fire of your love."

"Yeah, just don't sneak up on us," Cannon added.

A chorus of running feet echoed from somewhere nearby, as if in reply to Cannon's request. Cannon and I looked at each other for a split second of terror then took off running. The pain in my head was gone as quickly as it had come. Was it a sign that the end was near? My end?

At the edge of town we made a beeline for the shore. We kept looking behind us to see if we were being followed, but we didn't see a soul, not even a shadowy one. The moon was high overhead. My guess was that it was about ten o'clock or so. Still plenty of time to complete the circuit before midnight.

Our next stop on the pilgrimage route was Cloch an Chú, Rock of the Hound, on the southern coast of the island. Mac Gorra's book described it as a huge stone that had been cleft down its middle by the tail of a venomous dog trying to escape St. Colm Cille's exorcism of the island. I'd describe it as an impressive remnant of the receding glaciers from the end of the Ice Age. It was a massive block of granite standing fifteen feet by about twenty-five feet with a wicked fracture running down its face.

"How are you holding up, Arella?" Cannon asked as he helped me climb over and around the boulders littering the cove where the holy rock was located.

I forced a smile. "Good."

Cannon kept staring at me, no doubt waiting for me to try and convince him, but I didn't have the strength. I felt sluggish and numb since the pain had subsided in my head. When he turned away, I glanced down at my lifeline; it was still there, but barely visible in the moonlight. Would it last the night? Could it last until the Cursing Stone was turned on end and I could go home?

El, I know ya can hear me. Ya can do it. I have faith in my li'l girl. Focus on my voice and keep comin' toward me.

The words no longer seemed like a reverberation in my head. My father's voice was so clear I expected to feel his embrace. I looked to see if Cannon would react to the sound, but he moved toward our next stop without the slightest pause.

We finally picked our way to the foot of Cloch an Chú. I closed my eyes as I did with the other holy sites. Behind my lids I saw darkness. My throat caught, and I choked out a moan.

Cannon's arm was around me, supporting my shoulders. "What's the matter, Arella?"

I squeezed my eyes shut harder. A faint pinprick of light swam in the blackness. I concentrated on the small dot of luminescence, willing it to grow, but it merely pulsed a few times before it was extinguished completely. Opening my eyes, I groaned, "I can't see its energy. I'm unable to see its aura."

"Look at me. See if you can see mine."

I closed my eyes and focused in the direction of Cannon's face. Darkness crowded in on me. I took a deep breath, trying to steady myself and concentrate. A pinprick of illumination emerged. Reluctantly, it throbbed in and out of my senses for several seconds. It pulsated and swelled, brightening and dimming intermittently until, after a few minutes, it finally burned with strength. When I realized it lacked color, I gasped. It was completely white, the color signifying impending death.

"What kind of energy am I giving off?"

I opened my mouth to lie, but the words were lost in a sudden loud clattering of rocks. Cannon and I turned in unison to see two of Declan's accomplices, Keenan and Bryce, barreling toward us, hurling stones and curses with equal force.

"Quick, say your prayer and leave a stone. I'll delay them as long as I can."

"Cannon, no!" I was certain the two attackers would erase the last trace of his lifeline and snuff out his aura.

Cannon pulled my face to his and kissed me hard on the lips. My fingers clutched at his neck, trying to keep him from doing what I knew he was about to. Ignoring my silent plea, he pulled away and headed toward the enemy.

El, move forward now.

My legs moved without conscious effort. At the base of the great rock, I found a small pebble to offer with my prayer. With shaking fingers, I jammed the stone into Cloch an Chú's cleft, whispering the first words I thought of, "Lead us not into temptation, but deliver us from evil. Amen."

I chanced a brief glance at Cannon and his assailants. They were intermittently flinging rocks and ducking behind boulders, seemingly unaware of my presence. Crouching low, I made my way back up to the road and headed for Balor's Fort without a second glance toward the shore. Once on the road, I let the tears fall and ran like crazy.

The climb to Balor's Fort was strenuous, but unremarkable. By the time I made it to the end of its narrow isthmus, I felt wasted. I flopped down on the ground, my back resting against the hard chalky soil, an exhausted sigh escaping my lips. I smeared away the tear streaks drying on my cheeks. Almost there. It's almost done. I glanced at my palm. "I'm almost done," I said, studying the tiny dot of lifeline stubbornly clinging to my hand.

I rolled over onto my stomach and pushed myself back to my feet, grabbing a small chip of chalky stone before fully straightening. The wind whipped my bangs away from my forehead, and the scar on my temple suddenly burned like someone had branded my skin with an iron. I crumpled under the searing pain. After what seemed like an eternity, the pain subsided. Was this my end? Was all of the pain and discomfort, to which my body had previously been immune, gathering together for one final attack before I became impervious to death? Would I remain here forever?

I started forward, heading toward the Wishing Stone. I was determined to finish the pilgrimage no matter the outcome. I crossed my arms, trying to protect myself against the wind and drizzle, but after only a few steps, I stopped cold. Three shadows began to materialize ten feet in front of me. They ebbed in and out of the darkness, their forms shifting from vapor to solid and back again as if they were unable to decide upon staying.

"Leave me alone. I have to finish what I started."

As if in answer to my words, the apparitions melted back into the darkness. I stood frozen in fear, though my chest heaved in rhythm to the pounding of my heart. Breathe, just breathe. Gradually, my pulse returned to normal, and I forced myself forward again.

At the end of the land bridge, I stopped beneath the Wishing Stone and stared up at it. Silhouetted against the almost full moon, the massive boulder seemed terrifyingly alive. It stared at me with sightless eyes that made me shrink back in fear. I closed my own eyes, trying to block out its menacing image. All was black. Was there no energy here, or was my lifeline so close to disappearing that I was no longer a seer?

Opening my eyes, I tossed the sliver of chalk high overhead. It clattered across the top of the stone, and then all was silent.

"The Lord is my rock and my fortress and my deliverer…"

"Why, Miss Cline, I'm surprised ta hear that ya actually paid attention in my class." The words were followed by a pelting of condescending laughter.

I turned to see Father Dalbach sneering at me, his narrow nose and chin pointing toward me accusingly.

"I'm also surprised that ya believe all of the rubbish Father Cillian has been feedin' ya."

My sudden alarm must have shown on my face because the priest's smile widened. "Oh, aye, 'tis true enough that Tory is cursed, but do ya really think leavin' a rock and sayin' a prayer will save ya from our fate? Father Cillian was just tellin' ya another one of his stories."

"Why? For what purpose?" I demanded.

"So ya would find the Cursin' Stone and give it ta him. He and Declan had it all planned. We were all in it together 'til they got greedy and decided ta leave me out of it."

My paradigm suddenly shifted, sending my thoughts reeling like a tectonic plate sliding along a fault line. "What are you saying?"

His smile widened, exposing large square teeth. "I'm saying that I want ya ta help me get back the Tory stone."

I shook my head with indecision. Was he telling the truth?

El, I know ya can hear me. Your will is strong and so is your heart. Follow it back ta me.

Follow my heart. I stared at Father Dalbach's pasty face. He was still smiling, but his eyes were dark with contradiction.

El. The voice in my head was different, but still familiar.

El, my dear heart, we love ya so. Please, come back ta us. The time is now.

"Mom?" I whispered aloud.

Father Dalbach's face wrinkled at my words then slowly turned back to his stony smile. "Are ya hearin' voices now?" The priest's tone softened with pity. "'Tis a sure sign that your time is short. Come with me ta get back Cloch na Mallacht, and the voices will stop, Arella. I promise."

No, Arella! My parents' screams reverberated inside my skull.

A sharp pain shot through my temples. Clutching my head with both hands, I ran forward blindly knocking into the still smiling priest. Father Dalbach fell over with the impact. I didn't look back. I didn't stop. I just ran.

By the time I thought to stop, I found myself half way to the last holy site, Mearnaid and the stone effigy of Mac Gorra. I had been traveling by way of the fields adjacent Tory's road, in the hopes of avoiding anymore encounters with the islanders. It had worked so far, but my luck suddenly ran out.

A few hundred yards in the distance, a dark figure approached. I was in an open field with nowhere to hide and no more strength to run. Tears welled in my eyes, blurring my vision. Feeling defeated, I collapsed to my knees and began to sob.

"Arella, it's me," Cannon said, his hands gripping my elbows as he lifted me.

"How?" I grabbed his hands automatically and examined both palms.

"Still there. Barely, but I still have a lifeline."

"Oh, Cannon!" I flung my arms around him, sobbing harder. "I thought they had finished you."

Cannon gently loosened my arms from around him. "Naw, I was able to delay them long enough for you to get away. Then

I booked out of there as fast as I could and lost them by doubling back. When the coast was clear, I headed over here, figuring you'd be on your way to Mearnaid."

I stole an anxious look behind me, expecting to see Father Dalbach in pursuit. Seeing no one, I urged Cannon forward. "Just one more and then we turn the Cursing Stone. Come on."

When we arrived at Mearnaid, it was empty and uninviting despite the moon's light. The drizzle had finally stopped, and the sky was now speckled with a million stars. There was no breeze. I felt like an actor on a painted set, everything appearing realistic but somehow lacking authenticity.

Staring down at the narrow trail leading to Mac Gorra, I swallowed hard. This was the place that had shortened my lifeline to hardly the size of a dash. I wondered if I would be able to finish this part of the pilgrimage without erasing what remained of my existence.

Cannon cut through my sour thoughts. "Arella, maybe I should just climb down to place the rock and say a prayer."

I considered his offer for a moment but quickly decided against it. "No, I have to do it."

Cannon nodded and proceeded to lower himself over the edge. I followed after him, reassured by his firm hold on my waist. Inch by inch, we shuffled left, then right, then back again until we worked our way down to Mac Gorra's rock effigy without incident.

"See that," I said, "smooth as silk and easy as pie."

Cannon frowned at my nonchalant bubbling of clichés as he handed me a rock.

I placed the rock between a cleft resembling two human fingers, Mac Gorra's petrified digits. My eyes ran the length of the liar's image. For some reason I couldn't find any words to pray.

Cannon looked at me with eyes that blinked nervously.

"Say a prayer so we can go."

"I can't. I can't think of anything to say."

His voice rose with his anxiety. "Why not?"

"It's like he's listening." I looked at Mac Gorra's fossilized face. The rock's head was scowling at me. "I don't want to say the wrong thing. Besides I kind of feel sorry for him."

"Jeez, Arella, just say something to put his soul at ease then. Now do it quick before they catch up to us." He glanced at his watch. "It's eleven o'two. We're running out of time."

I bit my lip and tried to pick through my sparse repertoire of prayers.

May the angels lead ya into paradise. The voice in my head was deep, scary, and unfamiliar. I repeated the words aloud mindlessly.

May the martyrs come to welcome ya. My throat swelled as I dutifully continued to mumble each syllable.

And take ya to the holy city, the new and eternal Jerusalem. I finished with an Amen and collapsed.

In the moment of darkness that followed, I felt weightless. I saw myself leaving my body, floating above, untethered by the physical world. I was devoid of emotion, and it didn't seem to matter.

No, El! Ya're not done. It was my father's voice, but it cracked in anguish. *We've yet ta go ta the lighthouse.*

I felt a jolt of energy as my soul slammed back into place. My eyes flew open, and my lungs hungrily gulped air. I was slumped in Cannon's arms when consciousness returned.

"Arella, are you able to hold on? I'll carry you."

I could only nod.

I couldn't remember climbing back up Mearnaid. I didn't even remember the trek back toward Cloch Arclai. I must have blacked out because, the next thing I knew, I was sitting in the graveyard.

Chapter Fourteen

A hhh! Ahhhh! Ahhhh!"

"Arella, Arella." Someone put a hand over my mouth and pressed my body down into a patch of dried weeds, restraining me with the weight of his own body.

Kicking and punching against the arms binding me, I spent the little energy I had regained since collapsing. As a last ditch effort at escape, I let out another scream before clamping my teeth into my assailant's hand.

"Ouch! Arella, what cha do that for?" Cannon sat back on his heels, violently shaking his hand back and forth at the wrist.

"What happened?" I asked, rubbing my temples trying to clear out the fog that had settled over my senses.

Cannon shook his head. "You bit me!"

"Oh, I'm so sorry, Cannon." I pulled myself to my knees and grabbed his hand. I didn't concern myself with his bleeding knuckle. Instead, my eyes went right to his palm. Thank goodness! There was still a miniscule trace of a lifeline.

Cannon gently brushed me away as he stood. I looked around for the first time since regaining consciousness. "Hey, what are we doing in the graveyard? Am I?"

Cannon smirked. "Naw. I just needed a safe place to rest after carrying you all this way. I figured this was as safe as any. I don't think Declan and his cronies are planning another assault before we reach Cloch Arclai. That's gonna be their last stand."

"And ours," I answered ruefully. "So what's the plan?"

"Plan? Isn't that your department? You know, you're the brains, and I'm the brawn."

I sighed. I was fresh out of ideas. "How much time do we

have?"

Cannon frowned as he looked at his watch. "Eleven twenty -eight. Just over half an hour."

Great! I crossed my arms and lowered my head as I dug a hole in the soil with the toe of my boot. This was the end. How fitting for it to come in a graveyard. I might as well just dig a hole and crawl in.

We've got ta go ta Tory Light, El.

"What the heck does the lighthouse have to do with anything?" I shouted aloud to the churning darkness.

Cannon looked at me with raised eyebrows. "What are you yelling about?"

I felt my cheeks color. "My father's voice keeps telling me to go to the lighthouse. I know it's crazy, but maybe now's the time. Maybe I should listen to my father."

Cannon's face did not betray any trace of ridicule. Instead, he smiled, saying "OK, Daddy knows best. Let's go."

We didn't waste any time hurrying down the gravel path leading to Tory Light. Though we were careful to keep a lookout, I was fairly certain no one would be patrolling the lighthouse. They would all be gathered at the pedestal, ready to stop us from turning the Cursing Stone on end.

The light tower was dark except for its beacon. The mariner's guiding light sliced through the night's fog and rain like a sword slicing through the enemy. I felt a surge of hope.

"How do we get in? The door's locked," I said, remembering the last time I had tried it.

Cannon twisted the doorknob of the tower's whitewashed door. With a loud protesting groan, the door yawned open.

"How…?"

"Never mind, we gotta move," Cannon said as he pushed his way through the doorway. "Now what do we look for?"

I could feel the blood draining from my face. I didn't have

a clue as to what we should be looking for. I closed my eyes, though it was already pitch black in the building, and tried to focus. For what seemed like forever, I was unable to see anything but darkness; there was not even a pinprick of light in the blackness that engulfed me. I concentrated harder, sifting through the shadows of my mind for something to lead me forward.

Suddenly it came, just a flicker at first, but it grew steadily into a bright yellow orb. I shuffled toward it, my arms feeling the way through the nothingness. The boards beneath my feet creaked and moaned a steady rhythm of complaint as I moved forward. When I was within the ring of illumination, I felt a surge of energy ripple through me.

Crack! The floor beneath me buckled and sagged. The sound of splintering wood and fracturing joists shattered the silence. I felt my center of balance slipping as the weight of my body dropped. There was an agonizing moment of weightlessness as I was plunged downward. Bam!

"Arella!" Cannon's voice echoed through the hole.

The ground beneath me was hard and damp. I rubbed my back where pain from the impact was slowly surfacing. I yelled up into the darkness, "I'm all right, but I think I've found something. Cannon, is it possible that there's a tunnel that leads to Cloch Arclai?"

Cannon barked a laugh. "On this island, anything's possible. Watch out, I'm coming down."

The boards overhead cracked loudly. Bits of debris pelted my head and shoulders. I tucked my head beneath my arms in a vain attempt at protection. There was a loud thud and then the heavy sound of Cannon's breathing as he landed right next to me in the pit.

We helped each other to our feet then stood in indecisive silence. The tunnel, however, was not quiet. I could hear the rhythmic lapping of the ocean's waves ebbing in and out behind its rock walls.

"Can you see anything, Arella?"

I closed my eyes and concentrated on finding an aura. For a few moments, nothing came to me except a dull pain in my temples. I tried to focus on the sound of the ocean, adjusting my breathing to its rhythm. The tunnel's darkness slowly slipped away from me as a dull glow seeped through the black walls of my mind igniting my sight with a brilliant golden beacon of light. "Give me your hand," I directed Cannon as I reached out my fingers toward the sound of his voice.

His palm was warm and damp. It shook in my grip. I twined my fingers with his and started toward the channel of illumination. With each step, the sound of the ocean roared louder in my ears, and my vision became blinded by the growing aura. Were we approaching the tunnel's end, or were my senses being overwhelmed by an acute awareness of sound and light?

El, follow my voice back. It's time ta come home. Ya don't have ta be afraid anymore.

I took another step and stumbled backward in alarm as my foot landed on nothing but empty air. Luckily, I fell on solid ground, dragging Cannon with me. "But I have to end the curse," I whispered into the empty air. I opened my eyes and the guiding beacon disappeared.

"What's the matter?" Cannon gasped.

Untangling myself from Cannon's grip, I crawled through the darkness, groping the cold hard rock until it suddenly disappeared beneath my fingertips. "There's a hole."

"It sounds like the ocean is just below. You hear the waves?"

How could I not? The crash of water breaking on rock thundered up from the abyss. "I have to go down there."

"What! Are you crazy?"

A jolt of pain shot through my forehead. I gasped aloud. Cannon's arms were around my shoulders before the pain had a chance to subside. "The light was coming from the hole. This is the path I'm supposed to follow," I said. "We're running out of time. You have to get back to the pedestal to end this."

I could hear Cannon take a deep breath before he replied. "I'm coming with you."

I was silent for a moment before I answered. "Cannon, I don't want you to come with me. I don't know what's down there. If I don't make it back to Cloch Arclai, you have to be the one to flip the Cursing Stone. You have to end the curse if I don't make it back. Go back through the tunnel."

"No way! We're in this together."

I reached into the pockets of my raincoat. The two clumps of clay from the nun's grave were cold and clammy beneath my fingers. I shoved them at Cannon. "Take these. Give them to Father Cillian for me." I felt his fingers close over mine as he took the clods from my hands. Next, with shaking fingers, I took my father's locket from around my neck. "This is for you." I slipped the chain over his neck, kissing his cheek lightly. "For luck."

"What is it?"

"My father's locket," I whispered.

"No, I can't."

I backed away from him. "You can give it back to me once this is over."

He started to say, "Arella…," but his voice faded as I leaned back into the hole and let myself fall toward the light.

When my body hit the water, I was instantly swallowed by a dense, suffocating cold. My arms and legs flailed wildly without my willing them, as my natural instinct to survive kicked in. I felt myself being sucked down deeper despite my efforts to swim. Lights and colors swirled around me. I was dizzy and lightheaded, choking and sputtering water from my lungs as I struggled to reach air. The muffled voices of Declan and Father Cillian came to me through the smothering flow of water.

My father's voice drowned out the sound of the others. *Stop fightin' and come back ta me, El.*

I was instantly wrapped in a blanket of calm. I relaxed all of my muscles, letting the current take me.

Chapter Fifteen

E l, open your eyes."
Crek-crek. Crek-crek.

Light seeped through a slit beneath my eyelids.
Crek-crek.

My eyes flickered open at the familiar sound. White light and bright colors ebbed in and out of focus before me. I willed myself to concentrate and managed to force the mix of light and color into a scene of somewhat familiar shapes.

Slowly, I realized that I was in a room with cream colored walls. To my left was a window, pale shades of morning seeping through the glass. On the wall to my right was a watercolor, a seascape of an island floating in an ocean of mist. The colors were somber and depressing. Gray, green, and blue mixed together into a surreal depiction of a land slipping in and out of time. An overwhelming sense of loss pushed at the corners of my mind, reminding me of something, someone, or somewhere I couldn't quite grasp.

Crek-crek-crek. A rolling cart wheeled past the doorway of the room. A plump woman in a starched-white uniform and rubber-soled shoes guided it out of sight.

"Dear heart, can ya hear me? Oh, how we missed ya, Arella."

I turned my head. A woman with emerald green eyes and dark shoulder-length hair streaked with silver smiled at me warmly. Her eyes were moist with unshed tears, her ivory cheeks pinched with anxiety. She took my hand in hers. Her warm fingers felt nice against my skin.

"El, do ya remember who we are?" asked a man standing to

the woman's right. His hair was all gray, the color of slate, and his eyes were a dark chocolate brown, set deep in a ruddy face.

For a moment, I stared blankly at the two of them, not quite remembering, not really understanding. I wasn't even sure that they were referring to me. Was my name El? How did they know me?

The man's face started to go pale, and his eyes went dull like someone had snuffed out the light. "Don't ya remember your mum and dad? El, ya were in a terrible accident. We all were. Your mum and I escaped with just some cuts and a few broken bones, but ya weren't so lucky. Ya hurt your head somethin' terrible. Ya've been in a coma for six months. We thought we were goin' ta lose ya. Just two days ago, we had a priest come in ta give ya the last ri…"

"Thomas!" the woman cut the man off.

A sharp pain shot across my forehead. My hands went to the ache and felt the gauze bandage wrapped around my skull. I moaned, "Am I on Tory Island?"

The man and woman looked at each other. Hope seemed to flicker across their faces, lifting their expressions. The man nodded to the woman then bent down beside the bed. "El, we never made it ta Tory. We wrecked on the road heading north."

"Aunt Fi?" I asked, not understanding what he was saying.

The man rubbed the wrinkles on his glistening forehead. "Arella, Aunt Fi's been gone for years. She died when I was just a boy. We were headin' ta the old cottage she had owned. She willed it ta me before she died. Remember, we were goin' ta go explorin'. Remember we talked 'bout goin' ta the lighthouse."

The lighthouse! *El, remember the lighthouse.* I sat up, tubes and wires restraining me to the bed. I looked at the man in his tweed jacket, and suddenly I remembered. "Dad? Mom?"

"Yes, yes, my dear heart. We're here. We've been here all

along." My mother pulled me into her arms. She smelled of lilacs.

I breathed in her scent and squeezed her tightly. Tears of joy gushed from my eyes, tears stifled and choked down for too long. Soon the tears turned into sobs, and my body shook uncontrollably with a release long overdue. When finally I managed to calm my crying, I confessed the doubts nagging at my moment of joy, "I thought you were both dead. I was living on Tory. It couldn't have been a dream. It was real."

"El," my father soothed, "ya've been in the hospital since the accident." He pointed to the wall. "That picture is as close ta bein' on Tory as ya've gotten."

I shook my head, not believing. "No, no, it was real. And Declan and Father Dalbach were trying to keep me there. But Father Cillian and Cannon helped me escape before my lifeline ran out. Look!" I held out my hand for my parents to examine.

My mom and dad looked at my palm blankly. I pulled back my hand and stared at the new, pink skin covering it. I had no lifeline. In fact, I couldn't even see any fingerprints. My hand was smooth except for a strange scar in the center of my palm in the shape of a sideways 8.

My mother's voice was quiet. "Arella, ya were burned over twenty percent of your body. When the car flipped, it caught on fire. Ya had ta have a number of skin graphs ta your hands and legs. The doctors said it was a blessin' that ya were in a coma and couldn't feel the pain."

No pain. Maybe it had all been a dream.

"Hi," a boy's voice called from the doorway, "the nurse said that she was awake. Is it OK if I just say hello?"

My father turned toward the tawny-haired boy standing in the doorframe. "Yes, of course, Cannon."

Cannon! The boy's dark eyes and amber tousled hair instantly brought back a flood of memories, images of his aura flickering white and his face pinched with fear and doubt. Yet, here he was alive. He had made it back from Tory.

As Cannon approached my hospital bed, my father introduced us as if we had never met. "Arella, this is Cannon Fidelous. He was drivin' the other car that was involved in the accident."

Except for an ugly pink scar engraved across his forehead and a contradictory look of relief imprinted on his normally volatile features, the boy looked exactly as I had remembered him.

Cannon knelt down next to the bed. His dark eyes glinted curiously, no sign of recognition surfacing from their depths. "Arella, it's nice to meet you. I wanted to be here when you woke up so I could tell you how sorry I am for causing you so much pain."

"Cannon fell asleep at the wheel the night of the accident," my mom explained, putting her hands on his shoulders. "His car went left of center, hittin' us head on. He's been here every day since his recovery ta visit ya."

"Recovery?" I asked. "Were you hurt badly?"

Cannon's face flushed a little. He looked down at his hands. "Yeah, I was in a coma, too, except I woke up about three weeks ago. The doctors say I'll be ready to go home soon. I'm so sorry, Arella."

Instinctively, my hands reached for him. My right index finger hesitated for a moment, hovering over his brow, before gently stroking the new pink skin melding over the blemish left by the accident. I looked into Cannon's eyes without saying anything. His pupils held my gaze for a few seconds before he blinked and turned away. He stood suddenly, avoiding further eye contact.

"Well, all is well now that Arella has awoken," my mother announced. "We should go and let ya rest, dear heart. The doctors warned us not ta tire ya." She punctuated her declaration with a kiss to my forehead before ushering the men along with her toward the door.

"Cannon," I called, an unmasked urgency in my voice.

The boy hesitated in the doorway without turning around. My parents gave me a wary look but continued out into the hall. I listened until their voices faded into silence.

I had no idea if my time on Tory had been real or not, but somehow I felt obligated to express my appreciation to the boy who had been my ally in that strange place. "Thanks," I blurted out. "Thanks for, you know…everything." I shrunk back into my pillow, hoping for some acknowledgement of understanding in his manner or hint of recollection in his eyes.

Cannon Fidelous slowly turned. Squaring his shoulders against the fluorescent lights leaching in from the corridor, he walked back toward me. After each step, he paused as if each footfall required a great amount of contemplation. Upon reaching my bedside, he reached inside his pocket. His tightly clasped fist quivered as it emerged.

I reached out with shaky fingers, not sure I wanted what he was offering. A length of heavy silver chain dropped into my hand, trailed by a large T-shaped locket. With my other hand, I grasped Cannon's still outstretched palm. I couldn't stifle the gasp that escaped my lips when I saw that he, too, had the same mark of a figure eight on the inside of his hand.

Only then did I realize that it really wasn't a figure eight. It was the infinity sign, the symbol of unlimited time, space, and quantity. Boundlessness. We had been marked by the journey we had shared, a distance so great that the rays of light from its source had branded us forever.

I pinched open the locket. Inside was Aunt Fi's miniature of a sunrise. I turned toward the window, and there it was, mirrored in brilliant certainty, just outside my room. A new day was dawning, and I had returned to witness it.

I looked up to see Cannon's dark eyes reflecting my smile. "Cannon, I...," but before the rest of the words could flow from my mouth, he bent down and kissed me gently on the lips.

The rest of my unspoken words were quickly forgotten. My eyelids flickered closed, and my mind's sight ignited with pink and yellow lights that gave way to tones of green and blue, the colors of love, joy, healing, and balance. Best of all, there wasn't any trace of white light.

Cannon's aura swelled to a brilliant glimmer, sputtered for an instant, then collapsed in on itself, before disappearing into a single pinpoint of light. The remaining spark pulsed in one last feeble attempt at radiance before imploding into a black hole of darkness. Somehow I knew that would be the last aura I perceived.

Island of Tory

Literature

Discussion and Activities

Literature Circle Questions

Use these questions and the activities that follow to get more out of the experience of reading *Island of Tory,* by Regina M. Geither.

1. How did Arella feel about spending the summer with her parents on Tory Island? Support your answer with passages from the novel. Do you enjoy going on vacation with your family? Explain.

2. Why does Arella dislike attending the Academy? What rules do you think Arella would like to change? What rules do you wish you could change at your school?

3. Declan is very kind to Arella at the beginning of the story. What was Arella's first impression of Declan? How did her impression of Declan change as the story progressed? Have you ever had a wrong first impression of someone?

4. Arella hears her parents' voices, smells her mother's perfume, and sees shadows. When you first read about these occurrences, what did you think was causing them? What was actually happening to Arella? Have you ever perceived something and been incorrect in identifying its source?

5. Why does Aunt Fi choose to paint certain parts of the island for Arella? How does Arella use these watercolors to figure out how to break the curse on Tory? Has a painting or piece of art ever inspired you?

6. Tory Island is one of the few places corncrakes can be found. Why do you think the corncrakes were attracted to Arella? What did their sound symbolize in reality? Why were the corncrakes and their calls showing up more frequently toward the end of the story?

7. Why do you think Father Cillian offered to tutor Arella? How might the story have been different if Arella refused the priest's help? Talk about a time when an adult other than your parents provided advice and guidance.

8. Arella and her father seem to have shared similar experiences with Tory Island. Describe these experiences. Why do you think these characters underwent parallel events?

9. Why did Colin and Brigid decide to take a stand against Declan? Do you think their decision was brave or cowardly? Explain. Have you ever had to reject a friend because of a difference in moral opinions?

10. The lighthouse played a very important part in the story. What did the lighthouse symbolize? Why was it an appropriate gateway for Arella's return to reality?

Literature Activity Ideas

1. Create a travel brochure for Tory Island. Use the internet to help you find information about the points of interest you wish to highlight.

2. Create a map of Arella's pilgrimage around the island. Include a key with information about each important stop.

3. Create your own watercolor of a point of interest on Tory Island.

4. Make a chart or graph showing the aura colors Arella experienced and the people they were connected with. Explain how their behaviors and personalities matched the meaning of the colors in their auras.

5. Draw a Venn Diagram comparing and contrasting Father Dalbach and Father Cillian, Arella and Brigid, or Declan and Cannon.

6. Pretend that you are Arella Cline. Create a journal or diary documenting your stay on Tory Island. Be sure to include Arella's thoughts and feelings on each day's entry.

7. Pretend you are Cannon Fidelous before Arella's appearance on Tory. Write a letter to your friend in the United States explaining your arrival on Tory, your impression of the inhabitants, and your inability to leave.

8. The names given to the main characters of the story were carefully chosen because of their meanings. Look up the main characters' first and last names on the internet. Explain what the meaning of each character's name has to do with their personality.

Regina M. Geither grew up telling stories of talking animals, cursed treasure, and mystical lands. She is an avid reader, writer, and published author of the book *Swamp Stallion*, as part of the McGraw-Hill *Imagine It!* reading series. Along with being a writer, Regina is a teacher, a wife, and mother of three. She currently resides in northern Ohio.

Regina is currently working on *Cursing Stone,* the sequel to her first young adult fantasy novel, *Island of Tory.*

For more visit www.reginamgeither.com

VISIT THE LOCONEAL BLOG AT

www.loconeal.com

Breaking News
Forthcoming Releases
Links to Author Sites
Loconeal Events

CPSIA information can be obtained at www.ICGtesting.com
Printed in the USA
LVOW101514200912

299637LV00011B/182/P

9 780985 081706